Whistleblower

By

ALYSIA S. KNIGHT

Heart Dreams
PRESS

Whistleblower

By Alysia S. Knight
Published by Heart Dreams Press
Copyright © 2016 Alysia S. Knight
Cover design: by Kelli Ann Morgan @
www.inspirecreativeservices.com

The views expressed within this work are the sole responsibility of the author and do not represent Heart Dreams Press or any of its affiliates.

This is a work of fiction. Names, characters, place and events are product of the author's imagination. Any similarities to actual persons, living or dead, business establishments or events are purely coincidental.

ISBN:1-942000-16-2
ISBN-13:978-1-942000-16-7

Also available from Alysia S. Knight

୧ଓ৪ର

Past To Die For

Temperature Rising

Kare for Me

Blind Witness

Beauty and the Chief

Trail to Her Heart

His Governess

Her Brand of Trouble

The Ruins – Out of Time

My Spy

Where There's a Will

Aurora Rising

୧ଓ৪ର

To those who do the right thing no matter how difficult.

ALYSIA S. KNIGHT

Chapter One

Zan froze mid-stride and listened.

Wind whipped the trees. The storm was about to let loose again, as if the California coast hadn't had enough rain, but that wasn't what bothered him. Twenty years in the military, most of it in special ops, had honed his senses. He turned his head, scanning the woods.

He knew by the sound it wasn't an animal running his direction. Actually, it was an animal, the two-legged kind. The question was − who would be on his property, nine miles from the nearest town, in the middle of a storm, with the only bridge covered by a rain swollen river and a ton of debris?

His muscles tensed. He didn't like any of the scenarios which sped through his mind. He traced the trajectory of the intruder and shifted his path to intercept. A small rock cropping made the perfect place to lay in wait. The sounds of faintly labored breathing mingled with the light thudding of footfalls didn't mesh with any conceived notion.

Zan took a chance and stepped out of his hiding place just in time to see the human missile stumble down the rise. He caught the blur of tan leather and strands of mahogany hair, and barely got his arms open in time to catch the woman as she plowed into him.

His arms locked around her trying to absorb the force which knocked him back a couple of steps. The shock of her impact was wiped away with the feel of feminine curves imprinting themselves along his body, followed by a warm, feminine smell that made his heart jump.

The woman's head barely made it to his shoulder which made her about five foot seven or eight. It was the only thing he had time to process before the first strike came, smacking him in the chest.

Her arms were trapped against his body not leaving any leverage to do damage, but he felt like he was trying to hold a wildcat. She pushed and clawed at him. Zan had to tilt his chin back to avoid her thrashing head. Her hair whipped his face, bringing with it a floral scent which distracted him to the point that he almost missed the telltale motion of her knee coming up. He shifted to the side enough to take the jab in his thigh instead of its intended target. It was enough to jar his attention to the fact he needed to try to calm her down.

"Stop fighting!" Great, he sounded like he was giving orders. "Easy, it's okay." Zan tried to soften the tone and thought about letting her go. He disregarded the notion figuring, in her state of mind, she'd take off and was apt to hurt herself in her reckless flight. "It's all right. You're safe."

He clamped her tighter, forcing her into his chest, curving his body protectively around her. At least, he thought it protective. "No one's going to hurt you." As soon as the words were out, the thought hit him hard. Someone had tried to hurt her. Only fear could instill this kind of frenzied flight. "You're safe," he repeated, bending his head over hers so his voice rumbled in her ear. "I won't let anything happen to you," he promised.

Her fighting eased. He wasn't sure if his words finally sank in, or she quit fighting due to exhaustion. The power in her struggling faded. With one last smack against the wall of his chest right over his heart, her head dropped down to rest against his shoulder.

"That's it. I have you. No one's going to hurt you."

With a shuddered released breath, her body went lax against him.

"I have you." He held her tight.

She labored to draw in air.

Zan eased a hand up into the silky mass of her hair. He didn't know much about comforting women. His failed marriages were a testament to that, but he wanted – needed, to comfort this woman who was a stranger to him.

He was a born protector. It was one of the reasons he'd entered the military at age eighteen. Not some need to play soldier or to be a hero, but a need to protect, to make a difference, and he had, all over the world. Many places he couldn't even acknowledge. Now, something told him, it was important for him to be here for the woman in his arms.

"You're safe," he said again.

Her head shifted against him and came up when he lifted his. Her eyes were the color of amber, and he felt himself becoming trapped in them. Even when the dark lashes drifted over them and her head lowered back to his shoulder he didn't feel free of their enticement.

A drop of rain on his face jerked him back to reality. He looked up at the dark, boiling clouds moving up the mountain. Wind lashed the trees. The temperature dropped about ten degrees in a matter of seconds. Chills shook the woman's drenched body.

Zan used the hand in her hair to ease her away enough to open up his jacket, so when she settled back against him, she was wrapped inside. His shirt was immediately soaked. He ignored it, shifting his arms to lift her up, cradling her to him. She made no protest, just burrowed deeper. He wondered if the movement came from her unconsciously seeking his warmth and protection or if she knowingly put her trust in him.

He set off for his house in a long, ground-eating pace. The woman wasn't heavy. She had a lean, muscled body, but not so thin he failed to notice the curviness of it either. Still, he figured the woman worked out.

He went over the image of her face in his mind. She had a nice face. Her cheek bones were pronounced, soft, high, distinct curves that called for the caress of a man's thumb.

He missed a beat in his stride almost stumbling. What was he thinking? The woman was terrified, possibly hurt, certainly in need of help, and he was having fantasies of touching her face. But it was such a pretty face and those big eyes, not yellow or brown or even gold, but amber, deep and mysterious. He liked amber.

Zan gave himself a mental shake. It wasn't like him to become obsessed with a woman. And, she hadn't even said a word yet. He didn't know anything about her. He glanced at the hand resting on his shoulder. She wore no ring. Still, he needed to curb his thoughts until he found out what had happened to her.

With that firm in his mind, he concentrated on getting her home, out of the weather, and warmed up. She'd fallen into a stupor. Shock, training told him, and now she wasn't running to keep her blood pumping, he could feel the chills shake her body.

"My name's Zan Masters. It's going to be okay. I'll help you. I left a good blaze in the fireplace. We'll get you into a shower to warm you up then find you some nice dry clothes."

Following his training, he talked on using his voice to calm and keep her alert. Zan knew most of what he said didn't register in her mind. "I'll have you warmed up in a minute. You're lucky I was out checking on the bridge. You would've missed the house, and there's nothing else out here for miles. But, you're safe now."

He added the last because they were the words she seemed to cling to earlier. They worked again. He felt the feather-light movement of her hand sliding up around his neck, and the tilting of her body more into him.

He tightened his hold and lengthened his stride. He broke through the trees, crossed the yard, slowing to mount the rain slickened deck. He curved around the side to enter through the laundry room.

"Here we are," he spoke as he shifted her enough to get the door open. Inside, he paused, wondering if she could stand. Deciding not to risk it, he eased her onto the washing machine and still had to steady her.

"You all right?" He got no response. "We need to get you warmed up," he continued. "First, let's get these wet shoes off." He slipped them off her feet. "I better get mine off, too, so I don't track mud everywhere." He kept an eye on her as he took off his hiking boots. "Okay, I think a shower will be the best way to warm you up."

She didn't say anything as he lifted her back into his arms and took her down the hall to the master bath. This time, he deposited her on the bathroom counter.

"Will you be all right here a minute? I'll get some clothes for you to change into? You'll have to make do with my things. They'll be huge on you, but I don't have any women's clothes around the house." He hesitated leaving her there. She looked forlorn, helpless, like a half-drowned kitten. It was all he could do to pull himself away.

On his way to gather some clothes for her, he grabbed his phone to call the sheriff's department. To his shock, there was no dial tone. A quick check showed the battery level at full. Zan dropped the phone on the dresser. With the bridge under water and the phone out, there was no way to get his mysterious guest to town.

Before heading back to the bathroom, he grabbed sweatpants and a long-sleeved T-shirt then added a new pair of thick sports socks from a package he'd purchased a couple weeks earlier. The woman sat where he'd left her. Shock was still evident on her face.

Reaching into the shower, he turned the water on

before shifting to her. He caught his breath at the sight of her. It took all his effort to think logically.

"Okay, before we put you in the shower, we really should get your jacket off. The leather doesn't need any more water." He stepped to her cautiously, but it seemed unnecessary. She made no move to protest as he started to remove the jacket.

It wasn't until he moved to toss it aside that she reacted. Reaching for the jacket, she wrapped her arms around it like it was a security blanket. No, he thought. Eyes wide, her breathing increased, body rigid. Panic more than fear filled her.

"It's all right. I'm not going to hurt you. I'm just going to put this down here." He eased his hand back, tugging gently. Her hold remained fixed. Her gaze locked on his face.

"It's okay. I promise." For a moment, she stayed stiff, then her head made a slight nod, and she let him draw the jacket away.

"That's it." He kept his motions slow, as he draped the jacket over the hamper. "Now, let's get you warmed up." He lifted her back into his arms. She wrapped her arms around his neck and made no protest as he stepped into the shower with her.

A gasp burst from her. A shiver shook her body, then a sigh slipped free, and her head dropped to his shoulder. Zan understood the feeling. He hadn't realized how cold he was, but the water felt great to his own body. He lifted her higher to keep the water out of her face.

"Can you stand now?"

She nodded.

He let her slide down his body, gritting his teeth at the delicious feel of the motion. Either there was something very special about the woman, or he'd been out of circulation for way too long, maybe both. He caught the hint of her fragrance.

"Let's get your hair out of this elastic." Zan used his elbows to stabilize her against his body as he worked the band free. The mahogany mass fell free around her shoulders. He moved his hands to her arms, rubbing them.

Her body rested weakly against him. Shivers no longer shook her. Her head lay once again against his chest. Her breathing was coming so shallow he wondered if she'd fallen asleep.

Zan hated to move her. "We'd better get out," he said more for himself, forcing his hand to the knob, turning off the water. She looked drowsy when she gazed up at him. A smile crept across his face. "Can you manage to change on your own? I left some clothes for you on the counter."

She nodded. "Yes." The soft word almost stopped his heart.

"Then I'll leave you and go change. Just leave your wet clothes in the shower, and I'll come take care of them later. Take all the time you need. I'll be in the kitchen getting us something to eat."

He opened the shower door, looking down at his own wet clothes. He shrugged and stepped out. Opening the cupboard, he grabbed a couple of towels, leaving them where she could reach them. Without a backward glance, he hurried out, pausing long enough to grab a pair of jeans before racing to the hall bathroom.

There he stripped down, dropped his own wet clothes in the tub and pulled on his dry pants. He was back outside his bedroom in less than two minutes. Zan paused for a moment before going in. It was the need to get a shirt that forced him across the threshold. Nothing could keep his thoughts from the woman behind the bathroom door.

Who was she? What had happened to her? How'd she get across the river onto his property? The faint sounds of movements from the bathroom, spurred him to action. Ducking into the closet, he pulled a sweater randomly from a hanger and tugged it over his head. With his shoes on, he headed for the kitchen, trying the phone once more on the way. There was still no connection to the outside world.

A crack of thunder had his attention going to the large panel of windows and the darkness setting into the gloom of the cold, rainy day. His nerves crackled, not with the electricity in the air, but with a familiar feeling of when he was on a mission.

Danger was there. He looked toward the hall. He didn't know what hunted the woman but deep within him, he knew he had to protect her.

❧

Marley stood in the shower trying to figure out exactly how she had ended up there. Wet clothes clung to her body, but she was no longer cold. At least, not physically, inside she wasn't sure.

They'd tried to kill her. She couldn't believe it. She was a bio-chemist. Dull, nerdy. The only intrigue she got was from the occasional book she allowed herself to read.

Everything happened so fast. One minute she was content in her own little corner of the world, and now, she didn't know what to do. It wasn't a feeling she liked.

All her life had been controlled. Child protégé, teen genius, and being an over-achiever didn't do her a whole lot of good now. She didn't even dare call any of her family. They would be watched. She just hoped they'd be safe. She didn't want to bring this down on them.

She could almost hear her sister's voice. *"It's always all about Marley."*

Marley reached up to wipe away tears from her cheek and found her hand shaking. Okay, this wasn't getting her very far. She had to find help.

Her mind brought up the image of the man whose essence surrounded her. 'You're safe'. She clung to his words because she had felt them to be true. He wouldn't let anything happen to her.

For a minute, she bathed in the thought until reality

forced its way in. He couldn't keep her safe. She wondered if anyone could. Marley slumped back against the wall and pressed her hands over her face.

If her logic was right, they'd already killed outright at least once. Not to mention the other deaths they were covering up. She wanted to curse Galan Bone but couldn't bring herself to do it. Why did he have to leave a note for her? Why not send it to someone who could do something?

She drew in a deep breath. He'd sent it to her because she would do something about it, where he didn't dare. Okay, maybe that wasn't nice. The man was dead, but it was the truth, and it was time she started to do some thinking so she didn't end up the same way. It was only pure chance she survived until now.

With a glance at the door, she started to work her way out of the wet clothes. The towel was large, thick and heavenly as were the clothes. The man had been lean in the hips but she still had to cinch the drawstring up to keep them from falling off her waist and then roll up the legs a good four inches. The top she could've almost worn on its own as a dress. Instead of rolling up the sleeves, she let them hang over her hands enjoying the warmth.

A sigh escaped her as she caught her reflection in the mirror. Her hair was a mad disarray of limp tangles. Make up, well she hadn't started with any but knew she sure needed something to cover the circles under her eyes.

She looked a mess, which her sister would say was normal. She'd never been big on her looks, but she still had enough vanity to not want to appear in front of the gorgeous man who'd saved her looking like a drowned lab rat.

The comb on the counter was undoubtedly his. Marley only hesitated a second before picking it up. With her mass of hair, she preferred a brush, but beggars couldn't be choosers. She had absolutely nothing, not even a penny in her pocket, just a small memory card which would likely get her killed, and if she managed to survive, it would tear apart the company she worked for.

Taking one final look in the mirror, Marley decided she looked as good as she could. She opened the door cautiously. The empty bedroom carried only faint signs of the man who lived there. Keys and a wallet sat on the dresser, tempting Marley to check the ID. She shrugged off the idea, figuring after the way he'd treated her, she couldn't be so rude.

Still, she couldn't keep herself from looking around. She smiled, liking the feel of the room. The bedroom was so large even the king sized bed, with its heavy wood frame and matching dresser, didn't overshadow it. The only thing that could be considered out of place was the open armoire doors, revealing a large flat screen TV. Everything else appeared neat and tidy. Even the bed was made. She could appreciate that. She liked order.

The clothes in the walk-in closet didn't even fill a fifth of the space. There were two suits hanging there, but the rest of the clothes looked about evenly split between dressy casual and work around the house and yard.

Feeling uncomfortable about intruding anymore, Marley made her way down the hall following the faint sounds of movement. For a big man, he moved extremely quiet. She froze, catching sight of him in the kitchen. It hit her she didn't even know his name. He'd told her, she was pretty certain of that, but couldn't recall it.

Never really one to feel comfortable meeting new people, especially handsome men, she stood there uncertain how to approach. This man wasn't only handsome, he was large, with a powerful aura about him.

What did you say to a man who had probably saved your life, took a shower with, though clothed, and you didn't know his name? Add to that, if he knew the mess you were in, he would wish he'd never met you.

Locked in her turbulent thoughts, it took a second for

her to realize he was watching her.

"It's all right, come on in." He had a low voice, not gravelly, but a hint of rumble.

Marley found herself moving forward.

"Are you hungry?"

She nodded, knowing if she opened her mouth, she couldn't get the simple words out.

"Good, I hope you like chili, it's homemade. I actually make a pretty decent chili. Not too spicy. I hate to burn my taste buds off. It's just thick with lots of flavor. Here at the counter okay?"

Marley nodded again. She knew he was talking to help her relax and appreciated his effort. When he turned to spoon up the chili, she slid around the counter onto a stool.

Like his bedroom, this room was large. It opened to the family room with only an island counter dividing the rooms. A bay window jutted out to one side with a table set in it. Windows ran from the ceiling to a padded window bench on one wall of the family room, giving a great view of the outdoors. Unfortunately, the mountains were obscured by thick clouds and rain.

Marley turned back as he placed the food in front of her. "Thank you."

"You're welcome." He came around and settled in the seat next to her while she took a bite. She almost groaned with the sensation of food hitting her stomach, not realizing how hungry she was.

"Is it okay?"

"Oh yes. It's wonderful." She glanced over to find him watching her and dropped the spoon. It clattered to the counter and onto the floor. "Sorry," Marley gasped, embarrassed at her clumsiness.

"No harm done." He was already off his stool retrieving the spoon. With a casual flip, he tossed it into the sink and reached into a drawer for a new one.

Marley could feel the color heat her face and knew she

was about to start stuttering. She hated when she did that. Why couldn't she talk like she did when discussing chemical compounds or theories? "I, I don't even know y-your name." Fighting to get the words out right didn't help. Thankfully, he didn't comment on her difficulty.

"Zan, Zan Masters."

When he looked at her, she knew he expected her to say her name. "I wa … ant to thank you, Mr. Masters."

"Just Zan."

"Zan." She liked his name. It was different. Like him. "I've never met anyone named Zan before. Is it a family name?" Marley couldn't believe she'd actually asked the question without stumbling over it.

"Sort of. My grandfather's name was Zedekiah, my father Zeke, and I have a twin, Zac."

"You have a twin?" Marley couldn't imagine two men looking like him.

"Identical, though I'm almost an inch taller. He won't admit that though, says it's barely a half inch." There was no missing the teasing before he turned serious. "Are you going to tell me your name?"

"You might be better off if I didn't." It took her a second to realize she actually said it out loud. When she raised her eyes to him, she found him studying her.

"Are you in trouble with the law?" he asked without pause.

The question took Marley by surprise. She'd never been in trouble with the law in her life. She'd never even been pulled over for a speeding ticket. It took a second for her to answer. Her head shook negative first then the word came out. "No."

He studied her. She knew he was making up his mind if he believed her. It didn't take him long to nod.

Warmth spread through her that had nothing to do with the food or the temperature of the house. The look in his eyes took her breath, and she became lost in pale, ice-blue eyes as they burned into her. Her chest tightened. A wicked smile crossed his face as if he read his effect on her.

"It'll be all right." His voice rumbled over her, bringing a wave of tingling with it.

"Marley," she whispered but he heard.

The smile deepened along with the lines around his eyes. "It will be all right, Marley." There was no doubting the promise in his tone, and for a moment, Marley let herself believe it true while she ate. Silence settled over them so easily, it surprised Marley when he spoke again.

"The phones are out. The storm must be affecting them, and I'm afraid we're trapped here because there's a ton of debris that came down the river and caught on the bridge. It will take a couple days to clear. But don't worry, as soon as I can get a hold of the sheriff's department, we can hook up a line to get you across." He added quickly as if to relieve any fears that might have risen.

"Until then, I've plenty of supplies, and the house is built to be self-sufficient. Heating, power, water are all on solar cells that have a backup that'll last awhile. Plus there's always wood." He nodded out the window.

"This is beautiful. I never even knew there was a house back in here."

"It's about a half mile to the road. I like the privacy."

"Then I came along."

"I don't mind. Though, I'm still trying to figure out how you got here." He looked at her, leaving it open, waiting for her to answer.

"I-I got lost in the st-storm." The stammering over the words came back with a vengeance. She was a lousy liar, even when it was mostly the truth. She really had been lost or more correctly, just had no idea where she was going.

For an instant, the eyes watching her became glacial, and Marley couldn't meet them. "Do, do you mind if, if I rest for a min-minute?"

There was a second's hesitation as if he thought to say

something but shook his head. "You can use the room that's the first door down the hall on the left."

"I'll, I'll just stay out here if you d-don't mind." For some reason, Marley found she was unwilling to leave his presence.

Zan stood and walked to the window seat and raised one of the sections, taking out a fluffy throw. "You can put this around you." He dropped it on the brown leather couch which sat between the kitchen area and the large rock fireplace, facing the windows.

"Thank you."

Her course to the couch took her within a foot of him. He shifted slightly drawing her attention as if she wasn't aware of him already. He towered over her, with his broad chest and shoulders. The memory of being pressed into his chest surfaced with a wave of heat.

Clinically, she'd say he was a perfect specimen of manhood. Something inside her said he was more than just good-looking, which was a problem. She didn't have any experiences to draw from on how to handle a man like Zan Masters. He was way out of her league, but for a moment, maybe she could just dream she wasn't an egghead nerdette, and she could attract a man like him, because she was definitely attracted.

Slowly her gaze slid up the column of his throat, over the strong chin dusted with dark stubble. His lips were thick, masculine, and she itched to raise her finger to trace them. Her breathing picked up a beat.

He had a fascinating mouth. One corner twitched a little and lifted, drawing her eyes up to meet his, and the air caught in her throat. The clear blue eyes blazed back at her like the hot blue flame of a torch as if he knew what she contemplated and was daring her to act.

"You can trust me, Marley." The husky words wrapped around her in a duel promise. He would help and be there for her.

"You don't know me." She found the words.

"For some reason, it doesn't matter." He lifted a hand to smooth back a lock of hair that clung to her cheek.

Marley found she wanted to curl into the touch as she did to the man, which was a totally foreign reaction to her. Her eyes drifted closed as she fought for control. At the feather-light brush on her forehead, her eyes snapped back open. His face was only an inch from hers, and she wondered if it truly had been his lips brushing her and not just her imagination.

"Get some rest." He reached around her to pick up the throw, letting it unfold as he draped it over her shoulders. "Then, if you want, we can talk." He turned and disappeared into the hall.

It took a full minute before Marley could break the trance of staring after him and settle on the couch. She wrapped up in the blanket, snuggling into the warmth, dozing lightly.

It gave her comfort hearing him moving around. There was something in knowing he was there that settled her. Her mind recorded the sound of the washer starting, then him in the kitchen. She didn't want to give into the exhaustion chasing her and sleep.

On its own accord, her mind drifted back to the morning. It had started so much the same as any other. She got to work, checked over her specimens. It was almost noon when she slid the last tray of petri dishes she had been studying back into their slot and went to her computer to record the data. Finishing, the message notice caught her eye. She opened it.

If this message is delivered I am probably dead.

Chapter Two

Marley froze. "What kind of a sick joke," she said to herself then looked at the sender, Galen Bone. Dread filled her because he really was dead. Two days ago, there was a fire at his house. He'd been asleep and hadn't awakened to get out.

Her mind brought up the image of the fidgety man. He was barely her height with hair that always looked like he'd been running his fingers through it because he had, leaving it in a mad scientist look. He had a hawk-like nose and bushy eyebrows. He was so totally locked up in his work he barely seemed to function in the real world. Still, they had managed a kind of friendship. She read on.

You must get the file to the proper people, but it can't be anyone dealing with the Gladiator program. I didn't know. I am sorry to put you in danger, but you are the only one I trust to do the right thing.

A file and password were the only things in the way of a signature. Marley couldn't take her eyes off the screen. She wanted to believe it really was a sick joke but didn't. Still she reread the note once more.

Her fingers shook as she called up the file and entered the password. She knew of the project, though wasn't working on it, but she'd helped with some of the early development until they closed it off to all but a very small team.

Gladiator was the nickname for a drug they were

developing for the military to help boost strength and stamina of soldiers in combat situations. Her eyes flipped over the technical notes going unerringly for the most recent findings.

Ice filled her as she read of a test subject going into a mad rage, destroying everything in his sight until he dropped dead. Massive coronary was listed as the cause of death. The man's heart had literally burst in his chest.

The findings were glazed over as a missed defect in the man, but there were others. After Marley read of the fifth, she skipped ahead to the end of the report. Galen had tagged on a note.

To date, three men died at their own hands after going insane. Others had become what could only be described as berserkers and died from blood loss or heart failure.

Eleven men dead, twelve counting Galen, an even dozen.

Marley thought she would be sick. She wanted to deny it, to close out the file and pretend she hadn't seen what was in it, what the people she worked for, worked with, were doing, but there was no way she could.

It was why Galen had left her the file. He knew she couldn't ignore it. She just didn't know what to do with it. Her heart thundered, as if just reading about the drug's effects could bring on a coronary.

She had to think. It was what she was supposed to be good at, but the whole thing jumbled her mind. She took a deep breath to steady her nerves.

First, she had to copy the data, but there was no way she could smuggle out disks or a memory stick, and the computer system was safeguarded from sending out information. Security systems were tight. Without Galen's code, she would've never been able to access the program.

That brought up another detail. How long would it be before Galen's access was removed? It could be erased at any time. She couldn't risk waiting. Marley pushed her fingers up into her hair, much the same way Galen used to. Dropping her elbows on the desk, she glanced at the player that she listened to while running.

Snatching it up, it took several extra seconds to remove the tiny memory card because her fingers were shaking. Placing the card into the slot, all Marley could do was pray that the file would load onto the card. She held her breath and pressed the download command. She could hardly believe it when the transfer indicator popped up. Time felt like it stood still.

The sound of the door opening across the lab surprised her, and she nearly tipped over in her chair. Marley looked up to see Oscar Hymas, section supervisor over Gladiator, enter the room and almost panicked. Slowly, Marley moved her hand over to close the file, bringing her project reports back up.

Her heart pounded as the man headed her direction. Glancing back at the memory ports, she shifted her notepad up so it covered them. Marley erased the last line of notes and started to retype it in, ignoring the approaching man.

"Miss Reynolds." He stopped beside her, waiting for her undivided attention.

Marley looked up into his dark, beady, little eyes and shivered. It was a common reaction to him. He reminded her of a rat, even his nose twitched as if smelling her out like a morsel of food to steal. He made her nervous, always watching her.

"Dr. Hymas." She stressed the term doctor because he seemed to forget it when referring to her, though her degrees outnumbered his.

"I wanted to come by to let you know I considered you very carefully to take over for Galen. Your qualifications are most satisfactory."

"I c-couldn't leave my project on a broad based flu serum. It's too important."

"Yes, I was informed. I still wanted you to know I

thought of you."

A chill went over her at him thinking of her. She managed a swallow. "Well, thank you. So you're going on with the pr-project?" She stumbled over the word, her nervousness making her stutter.

"Yes, of course. It's almost finished. It will be going out to the military in just over a month." His pointed nose tilted in the air as he looked down at her.

"A month?" Marley gasped. "What of the testing?" She burst out then caught herself. "It can't be near completion."

"Near enough. The findings are strong. The military wants it."

Marley couldn't believe the man could callously make such a statement. She knew he would have all the information on the deaths. There were notes made by him as he observed the testing.

"We've a few minor glitches we're working on, but it should be released on time."

Minor glitches. She wanted to yell. *Men were going insane and dying.*

"Well, would you?" Oscar Hymas sounded annoyed.

"What?" Marley stared at him, trying to switch her thinking around to what she'd missed.

"Would you like to have lunch with me today?" His features tightened, making his face appear more rodent-like.

"Oh." Marley swallowed back a wave of nausea that came as much from the thought of having lunch with him as trying to smuggle out the file. "I hav-ve a dentist appointment. I have to leave s-soon."

His eyes hardened to black points. "Another time then."

Marley could only nod. He stood over her nearly a full minute longer before he turned and walked away without a parting word. Hearing the door close, Marley slumped back in her seat. She had to get out of there. They were giving the drug to the military in just a month. She had to stop it.

Switching the computer to the memory card, it indicated the file had been successfully downloaded. Still, she checked to make sure the information was all there before removing it, and shutting down the computer.

Marley started to return the card to her player then hesitated, nervous at the thought of putting it there. It wasn't usual for security to check her player, but it had happened. In fact, they had checked it the day before. She usually left the player in her car to avoid the hassle of security but had forgotten and left it in her pocket again today.

She thought of just dropping the card in her pocket then dismissed the idea as too risky. But it made her remember the small hole she'd found the other day in the pocket lining of her suede leather jacket. She'd meant to fix it last night but had gotten side tracked then ran out of time.

Going to her work counter, she found a tiny plastic sleeve and placed the memory chip inside and sealed it. With the plastic wrapped around the chip, it barely fit through the hole which was only about a half inch long. She worked the chip down to the corner where the seams met. Running her fingers over the seam several times, she was satisfied it couldn't be felt. With a last steadying breath, she removed her lab coat and pulled on the jacket.

Her fingers trembled as she reached for the doorknob. "I can do this," she said the words to herself. Her legs shook as she took the stairs three flights down. She should've taken the elevator, but that would've been out of character, and instinct told her she shouldn't deviate from the norm.

Like I'm some master spy knowing how to act. She took a deep breath. *I can do this*, she repeated in her mind as she approached security.

"Dr. Reynolds," the guard greeted as she approached.

"Hi, Mike."

"You left your lunch in your car again?" The guard was nearing retirement and had a warm smile.

"Oh, no." Marley dropped her keys and player into a tray. "I have a d-dentist appointment." She fumbled over the words, and for once in her life, was thankful for her slight stuttering problem.

"Have a cavity?"

"I'm afraid s-so." She held her breath stepping through the metal detector, praying that the small chip wouldn't be detected.

When no blaring alarm sounded, she almost sank to the ground in relief.

"Well, I'd say have a good day, but I'd better change it to good luck."

"Thanks, Mike. I'll need it." *That was an understatement.* She was about to reach for her keys and player when the door opened behind the security station. Marley recognized the security chief, Calvin Mills, a stone-faced, bull of a man. She found him cold and intimidating. His hand clamped over the player before hers. Mud colored eyes met hers.

"May I?" It wasn't really a question, but she nodded.

Marley's heart about sank when he turned the player and flipped open the memory port. If anything, his frown lines deepened, but the face was so immovable it was hard to tell. The man turned the device over and touched the power button. Marley could see the play list come up, and the security man scrolled over the songs. He took a full minute before turning it off and handing it back to her. He didn't say a word in dismissal as he turned away.

Marley glanced at the older security man. Mike just shrugged. Marley forced a smile, but when she looked back, she could see Calvin Mills standing off to the side, talking on his radio.

Marley made it through the doors and had to keep

herself from breaking into a run for her car. Unfortunately, it was in the back of the parking lot. Being a secured place, she always parked in the back, like she took the stairs, for the extra exercise.

She'd almost reached her car when she heard footsteps coming toward her. Marley looked back, catching a glimpse of the tall, smooched-faced man. She quickened her pace. Drew Jansen was Calvin Mills' right-hand man, and Marley found him even scarier. Where Mills was deadpan, Marley always felt a malevolent streak in Jansen.

Marley just reached her car when the man called out to her. "Dr. Reynolds."

For a second, she debated on ignoring the man but knew it was no use. "Yes." She turned back to him, clamping her hand on her keys.

"I wonder if I might have a word with you." The man sounded far too civilized, especially for someone who looked like he enjoyed pulling wings off of butterflies.

"What can I do for you, Mr. Jansen?"

"You can tell me what you did with the file you accessed. It would make things a whole lot easier."

The fear Marley had been holding back flooded her, and she fought for calm. "I'm afraid I don't know what you mean." Her voice trembled slightly, but for once, she didn't stutter.

"I was doing a computer sweep of Bonehead's files. I picked up the access and followed it to your terminal and found it had been downloaded," he glanced at his watch, "about fifteen minutes ago."

Fifteen minutes, had that been all? "I'm afraid you've made s-some mistake. I don't have access to Dr. Bones' files. I was on my terminal f-fifteen minutes ago, but I was recording data on specimen progression. Dr. Hymas was there if you don't believe me."

Knowing her bravado was failing, she reached for the car handle. "If you'll excus-se me, I have–" Marley broke off as a hand gripped her arm, jerking her back around. "Hey. What do you think—" She cut off again at the sight of the hypodermic gun in his hand.

The scream barely made it out of her mouth before he pressed the hypodermic to her neck. The world immediately blurred, and her legs dropped out from under her. A sinewy arm locked around her as her body was pressed against the car.

"Where's the download?" The words growled in her ear. Offending hands ran over her.

"Not here, you idiot." The words came through the fog in her mind.

She was aware of being shoved into her car and driven off, but everything remained in a haze. The car turned off the paved road and bounced over deep ruts before it stopped. A few seconds later, rough hands returned to travel over her. Marley wanted to knock them away, to scream for help, but nothing made it past the fuzz of her mind.

"Too bad," a voice wheezed out. "The Doc's got a pretty good body."

"Don't think about it. It's got to look like an accident."

"Shame." There was a pause. "I can't find it."

A string of swear words cut the air. "All right, put her to rights, and let's head back to the road." Marley now recognized Calvin Mills as the other voice.

"What about the file?"

"She must've stashed it back at the lab. We'll search. Either way, it will be destroyed with her. Just make sure you wipe any back door accesses to the computer as soon as we get back."

"Already done."

The door slammed followed by the sound of two others. The car bumped again over rough ground then up onto the road. It picked up speed then abruptly skidded to a stop, throwing her to the floor. A second later, the door was jerked open again. This time when hands pulled her out, they shoved her into the front seat.

Marley could make out Drew Jansen's flat features leaning over her. His fat lips pulled up in a snarl. "Sorry, Doc, it could've been fun." He patted her face roughly. Marley wanted to cringe from the stinging contact, but it helped to bring her more alert.

"We'd better hurry. She's coming out of it." The man grumbled back, studying her face.

"We want her out of it, so nothing shows up in an autopsy. Help me get this set before someone comes along."

A swear word burst through the air.

"What happened?" Jansen called out, jerking back out of the car.

"Rock rolled under me, twisted my ankle," Mills growled and swore again. "Help me to the car then you can push her over."

Over. Marley forced her head up and sucked in a deep breath. The dark clouds that hung over the valley below were not in her mind. She drew in more air and realized her car sat facing the curve in the road that dropped off several hundred feet. The motor was running. Her mind was still sluggish, but it didn't take much to realize they were going to run her car off the edge, and there was no way she'd survive.

Her first thought was to drive away, but with one look in the rearview mirror and the sight of the car parked directly behind her and the cliff so close in front, even her foggy mind knew it was impossible. Forcing more air into her lungs helped push away the lingering effects of the drug, Marley knew she had one option, run.

Another glimpse in the mirror showed Jansen helping Mills into the passenger seat of the other car. Knowing it was as good as she'd get for a head start, she took another deep breath and swung her legs out. She felt a little shaky, but it steadied quickly.

"The Doc," Mills shouted with his ever present swear words.

Fear and adrenaline burst through her, wiping away the last embers of the drug. Marley took off down the road. She could hear Jansen coming after her and forced herself to put on more speed, pushing back a hint of nausea that threatened to rise. If she could keep out of his reach, she knew she could outdistance him. She ran for pleasure, at least three miles every night and five on weekends.

The slope of the road was jarring, but she was putting more distance between them. Then she heard the roar of an engine behind her. Glancing back over her shoulder, she almost stumbled. Mills drove past Jansen who was bearing down on her.

Marley dodged, shifting directions at the last instant so the car missed her, but it cost her time. Jansen closed in. Mills put the car in reverse heading back at her. Taking the only direction open to her, Marley veered to the edge of the road, going over. The hillside was muddy from recent rain, but fortunately, it wasn't as steep or as far down as where they were going to push her car over. Still it was too steep to run down, so she sat down and slid.

She used her leather clad arms to keep branches from whipping her face and control her path and speed. It was a terrifying, reckless flight, but the sound of a man above her kept her from trying to stop. Reaching the bottom, Marley stumbled to her feet and took off running again, dodging trees, and wading through streams when they were too big to jump. Blood pounded in her with each step. Her mind locked onto nothing but running.

Rain came down in torrents. She didn't stop. Several times she slipped and fell, but after catching a couple breaths, she was back on her feet. Running again, without any conscious thought of where to.

Marley jerked back into awareness. The question

slipped through her mind as she opened her eyes and stared out the window. Rain still came down, and the sky darkened with the approaching evening. She huddled into the soft blanket and wished she could remain there, safe and warm forever. It wasn't the house that made her feel that way though. Her gaze shifted unerringly to where the man sat at the counter, going over a stack of papers.

She didn't know why he made her feel so safe, but he did. She bit the edge of her lip to hold back the urge to cry. Why did she have to meet him just when her life became a mess? Why couldn't it have been a month ago or even a week, when she'd have a chance to maybe get to know him?

Yeah, she'd probably get all tongue-tied and mess it up, and he'd go away thinking she was a moron. But, at least she would have had a chance. Now, she couldn't stay here and put him in danger. A wave of despair hit her. It would be dangerous for anyone that gave her aid.

ଔୠ

Zan knew she was back with him, just as he'd known by grimaces and tightening in her features she'd been locked in some unpleasant memories. Curled up in a ball in the corner of the couch, her nose barely poked over the edge of the blanket. Her eyes followed him, but she was silent.

He wondered what was going through her mind. From her reaction, he judged that she wasn't in trouble with the law. She'd been truly stunned by the thought that she might be.

She also made a comment that sounded like she had knowledge of the area, though she didn't know his house was here. Few people did. He liked it that way. Still, that indicated she must live locally, so he'd say in town or in the town on the other side of the mountain.

It wasn't much to go on. He'd just have to wait until she felt comfortable in confiding in him. Marley, he smiled, liking the unusual name then his thoughts turned pensive. Marley was in trouble, he had no doubt about that, just as he had no doubt he'd do anything to help her.

"You really should try getting some sleep," he said, without looking up, knowing her eyes were on him.

"No." It was said softly, and he waited for more to follow and it did. "I'm afraid to."

"You don't need to be." He raised his head now to look at her. "I won't hurt you."

"I know." She met his gaze from across the room. "It could be dangerous for you having me here."

He would've smiled if she wasn't so serious. "Who's after you, Marley?"

She shook her head, eyes wide and watery. "You don't want to be involved, Zan."

"I think you better let me decide that. Besides, I'm already involved. I gave you my oath that I would keep you safe, and I don't go back on my word."

The longing in her eyes was more than he could bear, and he stood to go to her, stopping when she shook her head.

"Is the phone working?"

The pain in her voice pulled at him, but he changed directions to pick up the phone. He wasn't surprised when there was still no reception. He didn't have to say it. He knew she got the message by the way she pulled the blanket tighter around her.

"Why don't you tell me about it?" He tried again, only to receive the same shake of her head. "You know we can't get out of here, and whoever is after you can't get here. So, at least for now, you're safe. You can get some sleep."

She gave a weak smile, and the blanket dropped a little. "What are you working on?" It was an obvious change of subject.

"Just some plans for something I'd like to build."

"You're an architect?"

"No, I actually have a degree in electrical engineering. This is a gadget I'm thinking up. Just tinkering my grandfather would say."

"You said something about building your house." She shifted on the couch.

"I did, from the solar on the roof to the flooring, with the help of my brother. I'm pretty happy how it turned out." He felt a surge of pride.

"It's beautiful."

"Thank you. We're working on his house now. It's about a quarter mile from here." A look of alarm creased her face, so he added. "He's not here right now."

"He lives here too?"

"He stays here when he's around, but he plans on retiring in four more months and coming back here. We'll get serious about his house then. We might be twins and a lot alike, but we have different tastes. We couldn't take living together for very long." Actually it wasn't quite the truth. He and Zac could live together quite easily and tended to stay close. They just chose separation so they could each remain their own man.

Somehow she read that. "You're close."

He grinned. "Yeah."

"I have a s-sister, but we're nothing alike."

"She's younger?"

"Yes. Julie is gorgeous. People always said I got the brains, Julie got the looks."

Zan had a problem believing that. Marley was beautiful. "So you were a smart kid growing up."

She looked almost panicked at his question. "I-I." She closed her eyes tight. Her face blazed with color.

Zan realized immediately when she stumbled over words before it wasn't just plain nerves. He waited for her to continue but she didn't. She sat there with a look of utter mortification on her face. Zan decided he almost preferred the fear. "I don't know whoever told you, you weren't pretty, but they were wrong."

Her head shot up. She gaped in surprise.

"Don't look at me like I'm nuts. I mean it. You're beautiful."

"I don't ev-ven wear makeup."

"You don't need it." He came back with the simple truth. "So you were smart in school. Did you graduate early?"

She nodded. "High s-school when I was fourteen."

"Ouch, talk about an awkward fit at college."

"I was a c-classic science geek, gawky with braces and glasses."

"Not to mention, at least four years younger than everyone else. Still the teeth look great, and I didn't notice the contacts." He wondered if that's what made her eyes such a striking color.

"I had corrective surgery last year."

He nodded, relieved that her eyes were her natural color. "So you're a scientist at Derrian Labs?" He should have figured it out sooner. It was a large research place on the other side of the hill.

"It's-s not that boring," she put out defensively.

Zan guessed she got that a lot. He knew a lot of guys that way. They would like the looks but couldn't handle a woman so much smarter than they were. Luckily, he didn't have a problem with that. "I take it college life was difficult for you?"

She shrugged. "Classes were okay. I always had the best schools since they first tested me. My parents couldn't have afforded it, but tuition, housing and a living expense was always granted so I'd attend."

Zan wondered if she noticed her stuttering was getting less as she relaxed. "So you went to private schools?"

She nodded, and he could picture her. She'd have been tall and thin, with braces and glasses, her head tilted down, painfully shy. Her mind going so fast, she was in her own world. There would always be a stack of books in her arms, other kids, all older, pushing past her.

She would have never fit in. A lot of guys would make her the brunt of jokes if they even noticed her. She wouldn't have been at the same maturity level with other girls, even if she far surpassed them in intelligence. She would have been an oddity, and different was never accepted well.

"What did you graduate in?"

"I-I finished my undergrad at sixteen. I have duel doctorates in s-science and chemistry, a couple masters and minors. I specialized in bio-science and infectious disease." Her words petered out, and she looked embarrassed.

He figured she usually didn't tell people that. "So you are going to cure the common cold?" He tried to make it sound teasing, and it worked.

She smiled. "Close, I'm working on a wide based flu vaccine that will counter most of all the changing strands and help strengthen the immune system so we won't be as susceptible to other diseases."

"Wow, you didn't take on anything easy, did you?" He was thoroughly impressed.

"I wanted to do what I could to help. Since I was blessed with this mind, I figured I'd better use it."

He wondered if she always felt it a blessing. "I can understand that. So when did you take up running?"

She looked surprised. "How did you know I run?"

"Several things. Your shoes are a better than average running shoe, well worn. You're in good shape. You'd obviously been running quite a while when you hit into me but weren't wiped out from it." He arched an eyebrow at her, daring her to disagree, but she didn't.

"When I started on my upper level classes, I had a roommate who was in sports medicine. Jackie kind of took me under her wing. Got me running, tried to de-geekify me, which didn't work real well because I still didn't fit in, but the running took. It helps center me."

It was his turn to nod. He shifted his image of her to how it would have been in grad school. She'd been jail bait. Even if any guy wasn't intimidated by her intelligence, he wouldn't have dared come near her because of her age. She sure wouldn't have had interaction with guys her own age. No wonder she seemed so self-conscious.

"You're very observant." For a second, he wondered if she'd read his thoughts then realized she was talking about her running.

"I learned to pay attention to things around me. Never know when it might save my life." He grimaced, seeing her tighten as his words brought back whatever danger she was facing. It still needed to be addressed, though he hated to bring it up now that she'd started to relax.

He wondered what she could've gotten involved in that would threaten her life. Surely it couldn't be that cutthroat for a flu serum. Then again, it was probably big money, and where money was concerned, there was danger.

"B-but you said you were an engineer." She stumbled over the words again.

He switched his thoughts back to her question. "I am. Actually, I also have two majors, electrical engineering and computer science. I got them while I was in the military. I just got out a couple months ago. Spent most of my time in special ops."

"M-m-military." Fear flashed back into her eyes.

"Yes, my brother's still in. We both joined at eighteen, right out of high school. Zach took another rotation, but it will be up in three months. He has his papers in to retire then. I was actually out on a medical leave then dumped my built-up leave on that."

"Medical. You were hurt?"

"Yeah, it sidelined me awhile, but I'm back to a hundred percent now." He thought that she was going to pursue the question of his injury, but to his surprise, she locked onto another subject.

"He's still in?" Panic filled her voice.

"Yes," he let the word out slowly. She looked like she was about to hyperventilate.

"He's in special ops, active in military situations?"

He eyed her carefully. "Yes, we were both over different units, but our careers pretty much paralleled each other."

She was off the couch, pacing back and forth. The blanket dropped forgotten, a wild look in her eyes. "We've got to do something," she cried out. Her whole body trembled.

Zan came out of his chair, grabbing her by the shoulders. "Marley, Marley what is it? What's the matter?"

Tears filled her eyes. She shook her head. "They're in danger. They're all in danger." Her eyes flickered over his face, but he didn't think she was seeing him. It was like she was looking at ghosts. He was afraid he was going to have to do something like slap her to bring her back to reality. When her head dropped to his chest, her arms locked around him, and she clung to him as if she was afraid for him. He closed his arms around her.

The clock chimed in the front hall. Lightning flashed outside, and thunder rumbled in answer.

Zan rubbed his hands over her back. "Marley. You've got to tell me what this is about."

Tears were her only answer, futile, heartbreaking tears that ripped him to pieces. Zan didn't consider himself good at comforting women and even more inadequate at understanding them, but he did know enough about human nature to recognize someone who had reached the point of overload. Whatever demons Marley was fighting to keep at bay were overrunning her.

Chapter Three

He tightened his hold. "Marley, I'm here," he growled out, not that it would do any good. Still she clung to him, sobs coming deep from in her soul. The thunder boomed, and she cried out as if shot.

"Marley." Helpless, he clamped his hands on her cheeks and forced her head up. Terror dominated her eyes, sapping the life out of the amber. "No." Clamping his mouth over hers, he kissed her in an effort to force life into her, much the same way he'd force air if he was giving CPR.

Her body tensed, and he eased the pressure, ready for her to pull back. Instead, she came forward. No sweetness or passion found its way into the kiss. Just an awkward demand for contact Zan happily gave.

He slid his hands up through her hair to the base of her neck where he began to massage the soft skin, working his fingers into the knotted muscle. With a gasp, her lips left his and her head dropped to his shoulder. A mixture of pain, relief, and pleasure groaned out from her. He softened the motion of his fingers, and she relaxed, her body picking up the contour of his as her legs gave out.

She made no objections when he lifted her into his arms and settled on the couch with her cradled in his lap. Her eyes were closed, but he knew she was once again alert to her surroundings. Thankfully, she seemed to have no fear.

He waited patiently until her eyes opened. The panic was gone, though touches of fear remained. He wanted to demand that she tell him what happened but forced himself to wait, afraid of shattering her control again. When she spoke, her question took him completely by surprise.

"D-do you know G-general G-gallup?"

"General Gallup?" he repeated, trying to get his mind around to where that could've come from. Surely she couldn't be seeing him. He didn't know much about him. What did they say about him, 'all ahead full Gallup'. No, she couldn't. The man was in his sixties. "I've heard of him, never met him."

She pushed her fingers through her hair then dropped her hands to lock them together over her mouth. "I need help." She looked up, pleading. "This is probably classified, but … I don't know what to do."

Zan felt his gut tighten at the word classified. At least it wasn't a personal relationship. He tried to look at the positive, but it opened a whole new can of worms. "I have a high level security clearance." He raised a hand to brush back her hair, caressing his fingers along her cheek.

"You'll w-wish you didn't know, but maybe you have the greater right."

"Marley."

"I, I need to see G-general Gallup or s-someone else high in the military."

Zan's muscles clenched. He knew he was about to hear what was wrong, and already it had him nervous. He forced himself to remain still.

"M-my company is working on a drug for the joint milit-tary. I, I'm not on the program, but I know about it. It's-s for use for men in combat areas. It's supposed to boost st-strength and endurance. It's to b-be released next month for field t-testing, but I need to st-stop it."

"Why?" It was the first question he could get out.

She worried her bottom lip with her teeth. "It's killing

people." The words were rushed with tears. "It can drive them insane. Turn them into bers-serkers. Cause suicides and c-coronaries. I don't even know how they j-justified starting human testing on this but they did. Out of a hundred and sixty men, eleven have died. They made adjustments but not enough. They're still planning on releasing it next month. They've d-doctored the data."

"You're certain?" Zan had to ask.

She nodded, accepting the question. "One of the scientists working on it was killed a couple days ago." She swallowed. "He sent me a message. It popped up today."

"Popped up? You mean on your computer, a preprogrammed delivery?"

"Yes, it said if I got it, they'd killed him. It gave me a file and password. It was all there, all the documentation of the deaths."

Zan didn't want to believe it, but the truth was there in her eyes for him to see. "What did you do?" He dreaded her answer.

"I copied the file then tried to leave." Her trembling increased. "One of the s-security guards stopped me at my car. He d-drugged me." Her voice rose with tension.

"I heard the security chief there also. They took me over the hill, off the road and s-searched me. They were going to run my car off the road, but Mills twisted his ankle and Jansen went to help him. The drug was wearing off. Th-they wanted it out of my system in case of an autopsy. I ran and slid down the hill and kept running. Jansen couldn't catch me. I just kept going."

That was an understatement, he thought. If she ran down and around the hill, that was easily over nine miles through trees, bushes and streams. It explained how she got there.

Anger burn in him. If she'd come off the hillside in the wrong area, she could've had a couple hundred foot drop. She was lucky to be alive. He tightened his hold, closing his eyes against the knowledge. He couldn't think about that. She was safe with him, and now he had to decide how to keep her that way.

He opened his eyes and stared out the window. Darkness had closed in around the house. He shifted his eyes to the phone sitting on the table. Its failure to connect had a new ominous meaning. It was possible that someone was jamming transmissions. Standard procedure, if who was after her had the resources. And, with the link to the military, they could, especially, if they were led to believe it was a matter of espionage. They'd come after Marley with every resource at their disposal.

He had to get Marley out of there. The bridge was no good. It was completely blocked. No way could he clear it to drive off, but like he told her, they couldn't get to her that way either.

He paused at the thought, a man could cross it. It would be tricky. He'd have to be good, but that was what he intended to do to set up a line for her. There was no way in the storm and dark to rig the line to get her over the river tonight. He felt her body limp against him. She was already exhausted. She couldn't hike back up the mountain in the storm.

Zan didn't like his options. Maybe he was being paranoid, but he didn't think so. He wished he'd known what he was facing a couple hours ago, before it got dark. Well, there was no going back in time. He had to plan.

He turned his attention to the woman in his lap. Her hair tumbled loose over his arm. Her lashes closed to make dark crescents on her cheeks. With her burden lightened by telling her story, she was asleep.

He didn't doubt a word of what she'd told him. He just didn't think she got the full significance of what she was facing. She might have gotten away from Derrian's security, but odds were they'd send others after her. Men trained like him.

The question was, would they use good men or hired mercenaries? He'd worry about that later, when the time came. Right now, he needed to get Marley down to sleep, so he could prepare for their departure at first light.

She didn't even stir when he stood and carried her down the hall to the guest room. Zan managed to snag the edge of the spread and pull it back without jostling her around too much. He felt a moment of reluctance to put her down, but he lowered her carefully, stilling when she whimpered as if distressed at leaving his arms. Unable to stop himself, he reached out and caught a lock of the wild mass of hair, rubbing the silky strands between his fingers

She wasn't boring, not at all. But, how did she get into so much trouble? He shook his head, trying to pull back but unable. What was it about her that got to him so? And not just physically, it was deeper, much deeper. Pushing away the thoughts, he pulled up the blanket and turned away. He had things to do.

Zan headed downstairs. Entering another spare room, he opened the closet. His dress uniforms were hanging in their protective plastic. On a shelf, his combat clothes waited.

He'd worked hard to put that life behind him, even went through counseling. As he picked up the camouflage pants, his mind slipped right back into it, going over the items he needed to gather. He shucked out of his clothes right where he stood, pulling on the others.

Dressed, he reached in and pulled out his pack. It was already loaded, but there were only enough MRE's for three days for himself, so he selected several others from the shelf for Marley. He didn't expect to need them, but you never knew. He added a spare emergency blanket then, on second thought, grabbed up his lightweight sleeping bag and hooked it into its place.

Punching in the combination on his gun safe, he swung the door open. He didn't hesitate at pulling out his holstered gun and fastening it around his hips then added several smoke and flash bombs. Next his knives, the first went into the sleeve on the backpack strap, and another strapped onto his thigh.

On the other ankle, just above his boot, he attached his second gun. He prayed he wouldn't need so much firepower. He didn't plan on killing anyone, but nothing was going to happen to Marley.

His hand stopped in the motion of doing up the strap. What would Marley think when she saw him? Well, best get it out in the open. Underneath, this was who he was. Still, it would have been nice to have had a date first.

Before closing the door, he grabbed up the emergency cash he kept on hand and stuffed it in his snapped hip pocket. Swinging his pack up on one shoulder, he snatched up his rain poncho for Marley. It would be huge on her, but at least it would keep her mostly dry and give her some camouflage.

Again, he hoped they wouldn't need it. Marley would probably think him nuts, some kind of obsessive, backwoods survivalist, but he opted for being prepared.

Going back upstairs, he paused in the doorway to the spare room. Light from the hall filtered in, illuminating the woman in the bed. He felt his heart lurch. Why was his need to protect this woman so strong?

He watched her. Marley slept the deep sleep of exhaustion. Her flight and terror had sapped her strength. She needed to regenerate. He'd give her what time he could but at first light they'd be moving.

Zan felt the urge to step into the room but pushed it back. There was still much to prepare. In the laundry room, he removed her clothes from the dryer, folded and placed them in the pack.

Her shoes and jacket were in the big room next to the fireplace. Zan ignored the leather jacket, going for the shoes. Deciding they were still too wet, he left them there.

On his way down the hall, he placed his pack outside Marley's room.

He stopped in his room to grab his wallet and then spent the next hour setting up simple traps, mainly to give him warning if anyone came near the house. He figured whoever came after Marley wouldn't think they'd face much opposition. He planned to use that advantage if needed.

Back inside, he made one final check of the house. Getting Marley's shoes, he went to her room. Entering silently, he placed the shoes beside the bed, turned out the light, and settled on the floor.

He knew he should've gone to his room but couldn't force himself to do it. Besides, the carpet was plush enough, and he was used to sleeping in a whole lot more uncomfortable situations.

Still, with Marley in such close proximity, his thoughts went to her. He could smell her soft fragrance. He'd noticed it earlier, raspberry and something he didn't know, but he liked it.

He closed his eyes and brought up the image of the woman. He liked that too. Trim body but nice curves. He wondered if she liked hiking and backpacking. Being a runner, she might. Her being brilliant didn't bother him, though he could tell by her reaction it did a lot of other men.

She didn't seem like an overindulged woman. That would've been a problem. He'd learned fast that high-maintenance women didn't appeal to him. He wanted a woman who'd try new things and not be squeamish if she messed up her hair or got dirt under her nails.

Not that he'd mind pampering a woman, he just didn't really know how. Marley might be his type. She just had to be encouraged, taught. She needed challenging a little. Yes, she'd meet challenges, Zan thought as he eased himself into a light sleep.

Zan opened his eyes, all his senses on full alert. He could hear Marley's faint breathing in the bed above him, but that wasn't what had awakened him. Someone was approaching the house.

He was on his feet in one fluid motion. Not stopping to notice Marley's beauty in sleep or contemplate his actions, he dropped his hand over her mouth, pressing down so any sound she made would be trapped.

Her eyes flew open, she tried to scream. Her arms came up to hit, bouncing off the tensed muscles of his chest. He calmly leaned closer. "It's Zan," he hissed in her ear. "Someone's here."

Her struggling continued a second more before her sleep-laden mind wrapped around the words, and she assimilated where she was and what was happening. Her hands stopped against his chest, eyes stayed wide with terror, but she nodded her understanding.

"Don't make a sound. Slip off the bed. Your shoes are on the floor below you. Put them on." He waited for her to nod again before he removed his hand.

He turned to the hallway and eased his pack into place on his back, strapping it down tight so it wouldn't hinder any of his movements. When he turned back, Marley waited by the bed. Good girl, he thought. She needed to wait to do as he directed. He motioned to her, and she slid across the floor.

Even in the darkened room, he could see trust in her eyes. If his gear frightened her, she didn't let on. She didn't doubt him that someone was there or that he'd keep her safe.

He leaned toward her. "I want you to stay low and follow me. If I hold up my hand like this," he made a fist, "you stop". "Slow, drop, come." He went over the series of motions. She nodded. "We're going to the basement. I've an exit there."

"I need my jacket," she whispered, leaning into him.

"Leave it. I have a raincoat for you."

Her head moved negatively. "It's important."

He'd searched it earlier and hadn't found anything, but her look seemed to say trust me. Well, if she trusted him, he could do no less. He just hoped it wasn't a fashion thing.

Raising and lowering his head, he flattening himself to the wall. She mimicked his action, staying close behind. He entered the main room from the opening closest to where the jacket hung by the fireplace. Motioning her to stay back, he dropped low, crossing the floor in a crab walk.

Reaching his target, he waited a second before he rose. His hand just clamped onto the jacket when one of the large window panes shattered around him. Zan threw himself across the floor reaching Marley as smoke burst into the room. He shoved the jacket into her hands as he passed, leaving her to follow him down the hall to the kitchen entrance off the main room.

He was about to motion her around the corner to the stairs when there were several thuds against the shatterproof glass and the sound of splintering wood. Zan crossed the room to meet the shadow as it stepped through the door. The intruder's arm whipped out.

Zan threw up his arm to block the punch. Letting the motion of his body carry him around, he sent a blow into the man, dropping him to the floor. Zan pulled a plastic pull tie from a pocket in his pants. Grabbing the stunned man's hands, he fastened them together through one of the stools hooked to the counter.

Smoke was seeping into the hall, but Zan ignored it. Catching Marley's arm, he drew her with him down the stairs. By the time they reached the bottom, she seemed to be past the shock. Zan released the bolt-locking mechanism on the small window and lifted down the whole window inset. Turning back, he noticed Marley had already pulled on her leather jacket and the camo raincoat.

"I'll go through the window first. When I decide it's

clear, I'll put my arm through. You grab hold of it, and I'll pull you up," he whispered his order.

She nodded.

Gripping the edge, he pulled himself up enough to do a quick survey before he pushed up and rolled out, flattening himself against the house. He waited to hear a movement. None came, but he knew there had to be at least one other.

How had they found Marley so fast? One of them had to be a heck of a tracker to follow a trail in this kind of rain. Rain might have made the ground softer, imprints deeper, but washed evidence away quickly. That's why they moved so fast, so not to lose her.

The faint rustle of leaves to his right, and the sound of one of his snares releasing, told Zan what he needed to know. He moved silently across the ground. At the side of the porch, he caught a glimpse of a figure, dressed similar to him in combat fatigues, but Zan had an advantage. He knew what he was facing. He doubted the other man, though cautious, had any idea he was up against someone with as much or more training than he had.

Zan came up behind him as the man watched the two side doors to the deck. Clamping his arm around his neck, he applied pressure, careful not to kill him. He held on until the form went slack. The guy would wake up with a massive headache, but by then, he and Marley would be long gone. This time Zan fastened the hands to the railing.

He was about to start back to Marley when he noticed the man's gun on the ground and recognized it as a tranquilizer gun. Deciding it might be handy, since he really didn't want to kill anyone, he did a quick search of the man for the spare darts, shoving the case into his pocket. He took the gun, going back around the house to the window.

He was almost to the window when he saw another shadow move. Zan brought up the tranquilizer gun. There was a faint hiss as the dart exploded out of the barrel, but it was too late of a warning. The man dropped. Zan didn't know how long the man would be out but didn't worry about restraining him, just checked to make sure he was breathing okay.

Satisfied, he went to the window. The instant he stuck his hand through, Marley grasped it and he pulled her up. She looked at him as if checking he was all right but didn't make a sound. He pointed to a set of trees to the edge of his yard and motioned for her to go.

She burst from her spot, keeping herself hunched low but at a run. Zan didn't have time to be impressed as he scanned the area for danger. The minute she reached her destination and dropped down, he was after her, running in a low, zigzag manner.

On reaching her, he motioned for her to follow and set the pace through the woods at a light jog. He hoped her eyes were adjusted enough to the darkness to keep from falling. He wanted to get as far away from the house as quickly as possible.

Chapter Four

Marley ran following Zan's form in front of her. At times, she almost had to struggle to make him out. He blended into his surroundings, like a ghost appearing at the shadows of her mind.

Her heart still pounded from his awakening her. Her mind raced over the day's events, trying to configure them to make sense, but they didn't. She'd never seen anyone, except in movies, move like Zan did when taking out the man who broke in. Zan hadn't killed the man, but she knew he could've and would've if he deemed it necessary.

She'd felt his strength of body and sensed his inner control, but the relaxed manner he exuded to her earlier had hid the hard edges of the man. Still, she wasn't afraid of him which was odd to her. He was the type that tended to make her the most nervous, but Zan didn't and she wasn't sure why.

Zan was controlled. It radiated from him along with power. His stealth surprised her, especially considering his size. He was a weapon with a conscience.

Marley ran. Her eyes had adjusted to the dark. Still, it was impossible to see anything. She just trusted that Zan knew where they were and where they were going. Bushes whipped at her.

Rain hit her face along with droplets from the foliage. She flinched when something dark appeared in front of her face. The branch caught in her hair, yanking it, but she didn't slow her pace. She set her breathing, in and out, letting the crisp, damp air fill her lungs, refresh her mind and invigorate her body. Running did that for her.

Ahead, Zan dodged a tree. She followed suit, but as she came around the tree, her toe caught an exposed root she didn't see in the dark. Marley managed not to cry out but could do nothing to stop her fall. Powerful hands clamped on her shoulders just before she hit the ground.

Zan pulled her up, set her on her feet and steadied her.

"You okay?" His voice cut through the darkness in a low, hoarse whisper. She couldn't make out his face.

"Yes." It surprised her she could sound so normal.

"We should be far enough away now that we can slow down, but we have to keep moving. In another hour we can find a place to wait out the night. Can you follow me?"

"Yes."

He barely waited for her answer before he started walking. His long stride made her hurry to keep up. At times, she wondered if she'd have to run to catch him. "Where are we going?"

"Up, over the mountain. They'll have the ways into town watched, so we'll have to bypass it."

"How do you know they're watched?" she asked the question mainly because hearing his voice helped push away the fear.

"Because that's what I'd do."

They walked on silently for a while longer until Marley couldn't take it anymore. "I'm sorry about your window and door."

"They can be replaced." His curt reply cut into the night.

"I'm sorry about the trouble I caused."

He stopped, and turned so abruptly Marley didn't realize he had until she ran into him. His hands locked on her shoulders, whether to strengthen his point or steady her, she didn't know. "You didn't cause this. You're trying to help."

Even in the dark, she could feel his gaze burn into her. His intensity was palpable. Zan Masters was a multi-layered man. He could be hard, deadly. He was full of honor. But deep down there was another side of him, the one that had taken care of her when she was frightened out of her mind. That man was caring and tender. He didn't intimidate her.

Maybe that was why she could handle this other forceful side of him. Forceful people usually petrified her. She had worked hard to overcome it on the outside, but inside, she was still insecure. She felt no such trepidation from Zan.

"Do you hear me?" he demanded.

"Yes."

"You're doing the right thing. Don't feel you need to apologize or thank me for helping you. It is my friends you're trying to save, my brother."

Marley felt her breath catch as the significance hit. Suddenly, the people who would die if she failed picked up a face – the image of Zan, his brother, his twin.

"You understand?"

She nodded then added "yes", when she could finally make her voice work. She understood. To Zan, it was his brother and his men who would be affected by the drug. He would do anything to help her stop that from happening. He would give his life to stop it.

Earlier, running through the forest trying to escape Mills and Jansen, her mind had dwelt on the risks. Now, with Zan, they didn't seem so oppressive, even though the attack on his house said the stakes had reached another level.

"We need to get going," Marley said firmly. The hands on her shoulders tightened in acknowledgement a brief second before he set off into the darkness.

Marley had no idea how far they traveled. She figured

easily five miles because, even though at the supposed walk, she was winded when Zan finally came to a halt.

"We can rest for a while under that overhang." He pointed to a dark shadow.

Marley couldn't see an overhang but didn't doubt it was there. She just went the direction he motioned, and ten feet later, the world darkened even more around her. A faint glow burst behind her, and she spun. The planes of Zan's face were made harsh by a soft glow from his hand.

He placed the light on a rock. "Get settled. I don't want to risk the light longer than necessary. It doesn't travel far but still could be noticed." He swung his pack off and tossed her a bundle the size of a football. "You can sleep in this. It'll keep you warm."

"What about you?"

"I'll be okay."

"Cold bounces off you." As soon as she said the words, she wanted to take them back. They sounded so waspish, but a smile tilted his lips.

"You in a fighting mood, Doc?"

"I can't believe I said that. It's not like me."

"It's okay. You need that. Use it." He turned his back to her, pulling something else from the pack. He disappeared into the darkness. "Make sure you keep your shoes and rain poncho so you can get to them fast if we have to leave in a hurry," he said over his shoulder.

Marley stared after him, her mind still back on 'use it'. How was she supposed to use it? What was she supposed to use? Shrugging, she picked a dry spot close to the rock wall to settle down.

Opening the bundle he tossed her, she was surprised when it pulled out into a full sleeping bag. She thought sleeping bags were supposed to be big and bulky. Figuring this was better than nothing, she worked her way in. She wondered what Zan would say if she told him she'd never slept outside before? As cold as she was, she doubted she would sleep but still this counted.

Surprisingly, she felt warm and content when he stepped into the lighted area. She hadn't heard him approach. One instant the space was empty, the next he stood over her. Wordlessly, he picked up the light, and it went dark. Marley heard only a slight whisper as he settled on the ground close to her.

"Don't you have another sleeping bag?" She couldn't keep back the question, feeling guilty for having his bag.

"I don't need one."

"So you said earlier, but I had your rain poncho. Aren't you wet and cold?"

"My clothes repel water," he said matter-of-factly.

"Oh. I've never slept outside before," she blurted out then groaned. She sounded like a nerd again.

The silence of the night sat heavy. Even the rain seemed to hold its breath. "You've never gone camping?"

Marley wasn't sure which was stronger in his voice, shock or disbelief.

"I've always wanted to go," she countered defensively. "It just wasn't my sister's thing, and I had to study. My parents wanted the best for me."

"Your dad didn't camp?"

"I'm sure he did as a kid. He grew up on a farm and went fishing as a kid. But we grew up in the suburbs of LA. My father works as an engineer at an aeronautics company. My Mom's a librarian. They were both very supportive," Marley added, needing to defend them, unable to take it when Zan remained silent.

"What was your childhood like?" he finally asked.

Marley felt a sense of relief when his voice came through the darkness.

"When I was little, I'm sure it was like everyone else's. I had a good home life. I played, got skinned knees. I took swimming lessons. I was even on a swim team. Normal for the area. I always liked to read and read quite early. I just started picking harder and harder books. I was curious, forever asking questions. So my mom started telling me to go look it up. And being a librarian, she'd bring me home books on whatever subject I was interested in that week.

"When I was in first grade, they bumped me to second and the next year to fourth. They wanted to go farther, but my parents said no, not wanting me to feel like a freak, but they gave me an accelerated curriculum. Still, I'd get finished and be bored. My mind tends to be different. Anyway, at the end of the year, my parents were approached about placing me in several different private academies. Finally they chose one."

"Did you like it?"

Marley heard him shift against the rock. She'd been asked that question before and usually gave her pat answer 'of course', but with Zan, she just couldn't. So in the darkness, with rain pouring down and men trying to kill her, she thought it out.

"For the most part, it was okay. I liked the ch-challenge. I felt special. But I also felt like a f-freak." The stuttering that had been absent for the last few minutes snuck back in.

"I was lonely a lot, so I w-worked harder to excel because then I got attention. I loved holidays because I got to go home and spent them with my family. My parents tried to make them extra special for me, but it caused problems with my s-sister. We weren't very close. She was two years younger and a decade ahead socially. She had the room all to herself until I came home. I felt like I was visiting in my own home, and she used to sh-shove all her friends and b-boyfriends in front of me."

Lightning lit the sky, illuminating Zan. He stared down at her. "Did you have many friends at school?"

Marley was grateful when the darkness settled over them again. "No, even in the private schools, I was kind of in a class of my own. The other kids like me were so into their studies that, well, they just didn't socialize."

"What did you miss the most?" His question made her think again.

"I always wanted to try sports, you know, like baseball, soccer, and volleyball. Volleyball looks so fun. But mostly, I always wanted to go to a dance. I went to one when I turned sixteen."

She let the words fade away as she remembered standing off to the side watching the other people and wondering what you were supposed to do to get to dance and even how to dance. After a half hour of watching and hoping, she finally gave up and went back to her room to study her chemistry.

Marley jumped, becoming aware of Zan shifting closer to her. "It's all right." His voice cut through the night. "You're nervous. You should get some sleep." His hand came out of the dark to touch her cheek. "Marley, I'd like to take you dancing some time."

Her heart pounded with excitement at the thought of dancing with Zan before reality seeped in. A wave of sadness followed. "I-I don't know how t-to dance."

"Well, I'm no Fred Astaire, but I think I can get us through it. Get some sleep now. We need to be moving in a couple hours."

The words brought back the memory of why they were there. A cold, icy shudder ran through her that had nothing to do with the temperature. As if Zan sensed her distress, his hand settled on her shoulder and remained there.

She liked the feel of the weight of it. Having him so near took her thoughts away from the madness, back to dreams of dancing with him as she drifted off to sleep.

⋘⋙

The rain had stopped, but for how long, Zan didn't dare to guess. A faint rose color tinted the sky, hinting of the coming sunrise. He looked down at the woman pressed to his side.

Marley, he didn't know quite what to think of her. She was as open as a book but still an enigma. She'd been in shock when he'd found her, yet gave him her trust. When the men attacked, she hadn't panicked. His violence hadn't frightened her either, and not once had she complained or even made a sound of protest at him dragging her through the woods in the rain and dark.

Part of him wanted to discount Marley as being submissive; like how she accepted the life she'd lived as a child. But there was more to Marley. She had the strength to leave her comfort zone, try to stand up for what was right, at the risk of her own life.

He heard the unease in her voice as she spoke in the darkness about sleeping outside, yet there was almost a twinge of excitement. He wanted to take her camping when she could enjoy the experience. He'd also like to teach her to play baseball, soccer and volleyball, but mostly, he'd like to teach her to dance. Hold her in his arms, sway with her to music.

It didn't really make sense to him, but she seemed to lure him like no other woman had. Was this pull what was missing in his other relationships?

He studied her features, captivated by the calm beauty of her in sleep. Even in the early dawn, he could make out her dark eyelashes on her sculptured cheeks. Her hair was in disarray again, tumbling around her face. He hadn't thought of grabbing something to tie it back.

The draw to watch her sleep was strong, but they needed to get moving. Having to bypass the two closest towns, they'd be lucky if they could make it to a town by evening as it was. Taking one last second to study her in the predawn glow, he reached out to shake her.

"Wake up, the sun's going to be up soon." He pushed away his emotions and slipped back into his authoritative demeanor. "We need to get moving. You have five minutes to prepare."

He stood, moving off into the trees to give her a minute of privacy and a chance to bring his own emotions under control. Keeping Marley safe was his responsibility for now. That was his focus. Not how she blinked up at him sleepily with those amber eyes or the way her lips crested when she smiled.

❦

Marley pushed her hair back and looked out into the shadowy world after the man she'd only known for a dozen hours but knew her life depended on. She wondered which was the real Zan Masters, the gentle man who had found and cared for her, or the almost cold and austere man who gave her orders, and instinctively, she knew could've killed if he deemed it necessary. She wanted to debate the idea, but there was no time. She had no doubt in five minutes they'd be moving.

The morning chill hit her as she slithered out of the sleeping bag. She shivered and longed to crawl back into the bag. Instead, she pulled on the rain poncho and her shoes then stepped into the trees the opposite way Zan went. When she returned three minutes later, Zan had the sleeping bag stuffed back into his pack, and any sign that they had been there had been obliterated.

"Let's go," he said abruptly, and they were off.

For the first while, the woods where wrapped in shadowed darkness, making her work to see where she stepped. Before long the sun rose, but it remained locked behind a heavy cloud cover, leaving an oppressive gloom hanging over them.

"I think it'll burn off, and we might get some clear sky today." Zan offered, breaking the silence after they'd hiked what Marley guessed was a couple miles.

"Where are we going?" Their trail was taking them uphill, and Marley couldn't keep back the question.

"Over the hills to the next town." He stopped and

pointed up at the mountain visible above the trees. "See that outcropping?"

She found the place he indicated. "Yes."

"If we get separated, I want you to climb up and wait for me under it. I will come for you there."

A chill of dread went through her. "Why would we get separated?"

"If whoever's following you gets too close, I'll lead them away and slow them down."

"Zan." Marley wasn't sure what she was going to say in objection, but it didn't matter, Zan didn't give her a chance.

"No, Marley. You do what I say. There is no debate. When I say move, you move. If I say drop, you hit the ground. No hesitation. You got me?" His eyes burned down at her, hot as coals in a fire.

"Y-yes." Her stumbling over the word seemed to soften him. His hand came up to touch her cheek in the barest of a brush that Marley felt through her whole body.

"I'm sorry, Marley, but that's how it's got to be. I'll get you through this." The gentleness came back to his voice.

"I know. I'll do what you say. I'd just like you to tell me the plan, so I know what to expect."

He held himself rigid for about fifteen seconds. Marley knew he debated over the thought of giving out information. He was used to giving orders and having them followed without question.

Marley couldn't believe the feeling of pleasure she got when he nodded. "Fair enough. How do you feel about mountain climbing?"

"I don't know. I've never done it."

"Well, we'll find out. That outcropping, we're going to climb the rock face above it. If we can do that, it will save us about four to five miles of rough trail. Okay?" He stiffened his body as if waiting for her to object.

"Okay," Marley said simply.

He stood staring down at her a second before he turned, moving in his long stride. They went another half hour before he paused and handed her an energy bar. "Eat this," he said, breaking into one for himself before starting off again.

They came to what probably was a stream normally but had become swollen to a raging torrent about ten feet across. They followed it awhile, climbing over rocks and shrubs, until they found a downed tree. Zan didn't say a word, mounting it, making his way to the other side. Not to be thought a coward, Marley followed his motions.

She swallowed hard watching the water boil only inches below her feet, but kept moving. Her eyes were still locked on the log for the next step when Zan's hands clamped down on her waist, and he lifted her off, setting her on the ground. Her head shot up to meet his gaze.

A smile crested his lips and twinkled in his eyes. "Pretty good, Doc, your first log walking?"

"No, I've done it before, just never with the water so turbulent and the log so slick," she added, when his eyebrow arched slightly. Defensively, she kept going. "I like to go hiking on some of the trails around here. I usually jog the ones down by the lake. This is just a little rougher than I'm used to. I don't have anyone to hike with, and it'd be foolish for me to go someplace like this by myself."

"I agree. Tell you what. I'll go hiking with you in future."

His eyes seemed to caress her face, and she felt the air catch in her.

"There's a lot I'd like to show you." His voice dropped low and husky with promise. For a second, his head dipped toward her, and Marley thought he'd kiss her then he pulled back, dropping his hands. "We've got to move."

He made it ten feet in front of her before Marley could get her legs working. She wondered if she'd imagined that

Zan had almost kissed her and decided she had. Why would a handsome hunk like Zan Masters want to kiss a skinny geek like her?

⚭

Zan couldn't get the vision of Marley's face turned up to him in innocent offering out of his mind. He wanted to kiss her more than he wanted his next breath. She was something else, not even hesitating to follow him out on the log when he knew it was way out of her experience.

He figured if he'd ever let himself be attracted to another woman, he'd look for someone who enjoyed the outdoors like he did. He just didn't think it'd be someone that he'd have to teach all about it. Not that he was thinking of Marley in his life. He tried to counter his thoughts. It didn't do much good. Marley interested him, from her resolve to keep up, to the gentle fragrance he could pick up as she followed.

He forced his thoughts on to what they were attempting. He needed to concentrate on getting a warning to the proper people instead of on Marley. It hit him that he didn't know hardly anything about what they were trying to do, except that Marley had said it had to do with a drug for the military. She said men were dying, and someone was definitely trying to get her.

Zan let his mind play devil's advocate and wondered if she'd told him the truth, or if she had just said it to gain his help. He quickly discarded it as a trick. He'd seen her panic clearly when she'd learned his brother was still active in special ops. Her reaction hadn't been faked.

He didn't doubt her, but they'd need more proof than just her word to stop the program, though it might be enough to get them to open up an investigation. Still, he wondered. "Marley, you said you copied the file. Will you be able to access it?"

"Yes, I have it."

Zan stopped in mid-step and turned to her. "You have

it? With you? On you?"

She nodded.

"They didn't take it before they tried to send you off the road?"

"They s-searched but didn't find it." A tremor shook her voice. He could see what the thought of them searching her cost.

Zan couldn't keep his own eyes from going up and down her body. He jerked his eyes back to her face when she shuddered. "Sorry. You have it still?" he asked again, unable to stop himself.

Again, she nodded. "In my j-jacket. I copied it to my m-memory chip for my MP3 player. They took the player, but I'd taken out the chip. I wrapped it in plastic and wedged it in the seam of my jacket. There's a small hole in one of the pockets."

He thought back. "That's why you wanted your jacket." He thought some more. "All right, we'll leave it there. That's probably the safest place for it. That was brilliant, Doc."

She blushed under his gaze.

He wanted to say more, what he wasn't sure, so he changed the subject. "I'm going to backtrack and make sure our trail is covered and set a false one. I want you to keep heading for the cliff. Can you do that?"

"Yes. I'll be fine." She headed off, leaving him standing. Zan watched her go, once again awed by her courage, before turning to retrace their trail.

CBEO

Marley forced herself to keep walking. She wanted to return to Zan. Though he didn't talk much as they hiked, she felt comforted having him there. She tried to relax. If she didn't know men wanted her dead, she would've enjoyed the hike. The rains had left the air crisp and clear. Water still dripped from foliage. The ground was muddy, but everything glistened with freshness.

The trail became rougher as she climbed up the hillside. She made it to the cliff face. Figuring she shouldn't be out in the open, she settled down behind some boulders to wait. She just hoped Zan could find her. The thought hardly crossed her mind when he came around the rocks right below her.

It only took him a minute to reach her. He slid his pack from his back. "We'll take a ten minute rest. Here." He handed her a small foil type package.

"What's this?" She studied the pouch.

"Breakfast. A food pack. They're not too bad. Go ahead." He motioned. "You need to eat."

Marley shrugged, opened it and started to eat. "What's next?"

"We climb. Do you have a problem with heights? I should've asked earlier."

"No, not that I know of."

"Good, then I'll go first. We don't have time and equipment to do a belay system so I'll tie you to me. That way, if you fall I can catch you."

"I'd pull you off too." Her protest came immediately.

"I can hold you. But if you feel yourself slipping, yell out 'falling' so I can prepare."

She gave him her first skeptical look but, after a second, nodded.

"Think you can make it?"

She glanced up at the cliff. "I think so."

An hour later, Marley felt the pull of muscle as she reached for another handhold. Gripping the rock, she raised her foot to a crack in the rock face and pushed her way up another two feet before repeating the process. Five feet above her, she could hear Zan and tilted her head back to look up at him. It was an intriguing view. He moved with cat-like ease, as if it was as simple as walking through the trees. Then again, to him, it probably was.

A sense of pride filled her. She knew it wasn't a tough

climb. There were plenty of handholds and not much loose rock, but she was able to keep up with Zan. True, she was certain he slowed his pace some for her, but not much. The first few feet were tentative for her, but she quickly decided she liked the stretch of her muscles and the adventure of the challenge.

She glanced back behind her. She also found she was definitely not afraid of heights. She felt a wave of exaltation at the view. They were about three-quarters of the way up; a good three hundred feet. Above her, she heard Zan move and turned her attention on her next handhold.

"Doing good, Doc."

Marley gave up trying to figure out if it was a question, compliment or a phrase just to keep her going. She decided she liked the way he called her Doc. His voice almost seemed to drop, making it a caress. Though she was probably just starved for male attention, it felt like an endearment to her. Especially, after he commented several times on how good she was doing.

"This is," she paused then, unable to keep it back, "amazing," she said finishing out the sentence.

"You are definitely a natural climber. I can't believe you haven't done this before."

"Me either. Even on my own, I still let work take over too much of my life. I thought I was doing better, going out running and putting in my garden, but I'm still missing out a lot."

"You like to garden?" he asked keeping his voice in the same hushed tones he'd encouraged her to use earlier so the sound wouldn't carry far.

"I'm not sure if 'like' is the word. I feel satisfaction in it and love the flowers. My condo doesn't have much yard, but I've made a wonderful place to relax and unwind."

"What else do you like to do in your spare time?"

"I like to cook. After I graduated and got my own

place, I took some cooking classes and found I was quite good at it. It's kind of like doing a chemistry experiment." Above her, she heard Zan laugh softly.

"I don't think I've thought of it that way. Usually, I'm thinking of it as something to eat, that tastes good. Guy thing, but I'm not bad in the kitchen."

"Your chili was good."

"Thank you." He was silent a minute then asked. "Tell me about your sister. Does she still live at home?"

"No, she married right after high school. Julie and her husband live not far from my parents. Her husband manages one of his father's car dealerships. They have a little girl now. Julie is the complete opposite of me. She takes after my mother's side, while I take after my father's. She's petite, blonde and peppy. She can play the helpless airhead very well, but she's not."

"What's the old term," Zan volunteered, "valley-girl?"

Marley laughed. "Actually, yes. But everyone liked Julie. She was on the drill team and was homecoming queen."

"Well, if it makes any difference, I think I'd find–" Zan stopped talking in mid-sentence and froze. Marley followed suit. She listened, trying to detect what alarmed him. Her mind barely registered the faint sound before Zan's order came. "Three feet to your right is a ledge, get there, now."

Marley didn't hesitate. She shifted directions in climbing. Out of the corner of her eye, she saw Zan push off the mountainside and make a leap for the ledge. In one motion, he landed and stretched out his hand for her. Marley reached out for him. He caught her wrist and pulled her up onto the rock outcropping.

"Down."

Chapter Five

He shoved her as she dropped. Rolling her over, he wedged her body back in the corner. His body came down over her. One arm snaked its way under her head, creating a headrest, forcing her face against his neck, while wrapping his forearm over her hair. Zan curled his other arm up over his own head to hide his hair and shifted his body slightly to better align their bodies.

Marley couldn't keep in her gasp at the feel of the hard planes of his body pressed into her.

"It's okay." His breath stirred the hair at her temples. He shifted again, trapping her feet between his legs.

Marley could now make out the sound of a helicopter and understood he was trying to cover her gym shoes. She pointed her toes out to flatten them against the muscle-corded limbs.

"Good girl. Now stay still."

Stay still! She was afraid to breath. People in a helicopter were searching almost directly above them, and, she was in the most intimate contact with a man she'd ever been in in her life. She wanted to laugh at the absurdity of it. She wondered what Zan would say. The thought dropped away as the sound of the helicopter came closer, and the edge of hysterics dug deeper. If they were seen, they'd be trapped. She shivered at the thought.

Zan shifted his head slightly so that his chin pressed against her temple. He whispered her name but if he said anything else it was drowned out by the sound of the helicopter coming closer to the cliff.

Marley clamped her eyes shut and held her breath as dust filled the air. She dug her fingers into Zan's shirt, pulling him tighter down, pressing her face into his neck. Small pebbles dislodged by the wind from the rotator blades peppered around them. Marley felt Zan flinch and guessed a bigger rock struck him.

His arms tightened around their heads, but he made no other movement. Marley bit down on her lip to keep from crying out. Seconds seemed to take hours to pass before the helicopter moved away.

"Wait."

Marley didn't need his command. She wasn't going to move until he told her. Her breaths were labored from being pinned down by his weight. She didn't care. Zan was security.

As the dust settled, she became aware of his scent – musky, masculine, male. It was familiar, and she relaxed but didn't loosen her hold. Above her, Zan too relaxed, though he didn't move other than his hands that burrowed into her hair.

∝≈

Zan lowered his arm from over his head and went to push up only to find Marley's hands were fisted in his shirt and arms locked so tight, he couldn't move without taking her with him. He tried to ease off her, but she tightened her hold. He managed to get a look at her face. Her eyes were shut.

"Marley, it's okay now. You can release me." When he tried to move, it remained impossible. "Marley." He touched her cheek, running his thumb over her smooth skin. "Come on Marley, open your eyes. You can do this. I need to make sure they are gone, and we need to get to the top, in case they come back. We can't afford to be trapped here. Understand?"

He felt the intake of breath against the entire length of his body, then she opened those incredible amber eyes, and he was trapped in their honeyed depth. Fear and trust wrapped around him in one.

"Marley." Her name was torn from him in a groan. Unable to stop himself, he dropped his head, taking her slightly open mouth with the storm that raged through him, spurred by adrenaline and the feel of Marley pressed so intimately along him. He detected her little gasp then her untutored lips followed his in the dance of tasting and caressing.

She was as sweet as the honey of her eyes, and he wanted to feast on her forever. For a moment, there was only Marley, then a rock bit into the skin of his arm, and reality burst back on him.

"No." He ripped his mouth away and shoved up in one movement. He knelt over her, gulping in the air that had escaped him.

Marley's eyes were open and dazed. Her breathing was just as labored as his. Her lips were full and rosy from his kisses. As he watched, her tongue came out and touched them in a light caress. It was a tempting but innocent gesture. He wondered if she could taste him there. Her taste was branded on him, and he wanted to drink again.

"No!" He forced out again, tearing his eyes from her, scanning the area. Never had he lost focus in a dangerous situation. He wanted to tell himself it was from being out of the military that his instinct had gotten lax, but he knew that wasn't it. Marley pulled at him as she had since he first laid eyes on her, even before he knew her name.

"I'm sorry—" His apology didn't get far.

"No!" She cut him off.

Her hand locked on his arm. He didn't want to look back at her but couldn't stop himself. She was up on one elbow. Her hair was an array of wild waves of mahogany around her face. But again, it was her eyes that held him.

This time, they glowed like molten gold.

"Don't you dare apologize." There was no stuttering of the words, but it was as if she had to force them out each individually.

"Marley," his voice softened on its own accord.

"No." Her fingers shot out to cover his lips, her head shaking. "Do not apologize. I have never been kissed like that. Don't you dare ruin it by apologizing."

Reaching up, he caught her fingers, pulling them away from his mouth but not releasing them. "It's not safe," he started to explain but she took over.

"No, it's not. I've realized I might die. But for fifteen seconds of my life, I felt desirable. Please don't take that away from me." Pleading was strong in her voice.

"It was a lot more than fifteen seconds." Zan didn't realize he said the words aloud until the shocked looked and color blossomed on her face.

"I ..."

This time, he knew the words wouldn't come out because she was flustered.

"We'll talk more about you being desirable later, since I find you utterly so. For now, I plan on doing everything I can to keep you alive. And that means not kissing you, because I can't think of anything else when I do." He felt satisfaction at the stunned expression on her face.

"Come on, we need to get to the top." He used his hold on her fingers to help her up. At the last moment before releasing them, he brought her fingers to his lips brushing them lightly. Zan turned, reaching for a handhold, pulling himself up.

❧

Marley couldn't take her eyes off the man who had just rocked her world. Zan Masters thought she was desirable. She wouldn't have believed him, except she could still feel the hunger in his lips on hers. She hoped it wasn't just her imagination because she knew she'd never shake him from the place he had burrowed so easily in her heart.

The rope on her waist gave a little tug bring her back to reality and reminding her she was supposed to be climbing. She managed a deep breath then followed after him, surprised at how rejuvenated she felt.

It was only another twenty minutes until they reached the top. Once again, Zan's hand extended down to pull her up over the edge. He released it as soon as she made it to her feet.

"Over there." He hurried her to the cover of some trees. "You okay?" he asked, working on untying the rope, not even looking toward her.

"Yes." She followed his actions, releasing the rope from her own waist.

"Thanks." He finally looked up at her. His gaze shifted away from her then came back. "Marley, I don't want you to think you owe me anything for helping you."

"What?" She stared at him in utter disbelief. "You th-think."

"Look, I … we better go. We've still got a long way." Zan turned and headed off through the trees in his normal ground-eating pace.

Marley wanted to smack him. Wanted to yell and throw a tantrum. Why couldn't she be more like her sister? It always worked for her. The man had said she was desirable. She'd never understand men. Her shoulders dropped in resignation.

She always thought tantrums were foolish and childish. Catching a brief glance as he disappeared amongst the trees, she knew for once she really wanted to be childish. Could he really think she'd kissed him out of gratitude? She opened her mouth to scream, but at the last second kept it in, remembering that there were people after them.

"Marley." Her name came in a hoarse bark, spurring her into motion. She darted after him fuming inside.

಄಄

Zan couldn't believe he'd kissed her. He had totally lost it. Forgot all about where they were, the people after them, the danger. All he'd thought of was Marley. Not keeping her safe but that she was his.

It was a good thing he was retired. He'd lost his edge. He couldn't believe it. When had it happened? When he was injured? He hadn't felt it. He'd just felt that it was time, that something else was waiting out there for him, and he needed a change.

All he could say was it was a good thing he'd gotten out before he put his men in danger. He tried to clear his thoughts and focus on his surroundings. He could hear Marley about ten feet behind him.

She was keeping up fine, but he had to get Marley somewhere where they could keep her safe, because he sure couldn't. He couldn't keep the thought of her lips from his mind. He wanted to kiss her again and again.

She'd let him kiss her. Not just let him kiss her, she'd kissed him back. It was obvious she hadn't kissed many men. Even if she hadn't said what she did, he'd have known. But she had knocked his socks off as his grandmother would have said. His grandfather would've laughed and said it was a good thing he had his boots laced on so he hadn't lost them.

He wanted to believe she hadn't kissed him out of gratitude, did believe it. Still, he had to keep his thoughts in line. He forced his thoughts to go over all the details of the trail. They'd follow the tree line, keeping in cover for about two miles before breaking down the other side, through the next valley. The river on the other side would probably be a bit tricky to cross. It was wider and carved its way through the valley.

He debated shifting and heading back toward the town just over the ridge, but he knew they'd never make it. It'd be locked up tight. No, they'd keep heading the way they were, as if headed for town, then shift, cross the next valley and drop into the town there. He'd see if he couldn't find a vehicle for sale, then put some distance between them and the people hunting Marley and get help.

He glanced back. She was there, and utterly amazing in the way she faced the challenge, and if he didn't miss his guess, she was also still mad. Well, good. She could use the energy it brought. And it served her right.

How could she doubt she was desirable? He just really hoped her feelings for him weren't locked in gratitude. He envisioned the fire in her eyes when she thought he had suggested it and grinned. No, it wasn't just gratitude. Marley was attracted to him. And, she was still ready to hit him.

⋘⋙

Marley still wanted to smack him hours later when they crested the hill and dropped down into the valley. She just didn't have the breath to do it. So much for thinking what great shape she was in. If Zan didn't stop and let her get some rest soon, she was going to smack him for that, though she didn't know how she'd catch him to do it. The man was like an automaton. No cancel that. He was a super soldier.

She shivered as it brought up thoughts of Gladiator. That had to be stopped. It couldn't be allowed to be used on any more people, on Zan's brother. Marley forced back tears that wanted to rise as she pictured Zan dead like the men in the reports.

She couldn't believe what they were doing – people she worked with. She thought of all the people on the program. She knew, when it started out, there'd been about a dozen people. Last year, they cut it down to just four. Shouldn't that have been a red flag when it was such an important project? No, a couple were like her, who had their own projects, and were just part timers on it. Dr. Hutchkins had retired, and Dr. Seaver was killed in a car accident while on vacation. She stumbled.

"Marley." Zan caught her arm.

She looked up into his worried expression. "Did they kill Dr. Seaver, too?"

"What?" Confusion crossed Zan's face.

She understood the feeling. It was how she felt. It all seemed so unreal. It couldn't be happening, but it was. The tears she held back filled her eyes. "Dr. Seaver, he went on vacation with his wife about six months ago. They were an older couple. She worked as a research assistant at the lab. They had no children. Their car when off a steep embankment and they were both killed." The similarities of how her death would've looked if Mills and Jansen had succeeded came to her mind. Her breathing quickened and tears burned her eyes.

"Marley, you can't think about it." He gripped her wrists, pulling her attention to him.

"How can I not?" she cried as pain hit her.

"Marley, suck it up."

If it wasn't so absurd, she would have thought there was a touch of panic in his eyes.

He gave her a little shake. "Marley."

She forced in a breath and swallowed back the tears. "I'm okay." She got herself together, forcing it to be so.

Zan studied her a moment before he nodded and released her. "Why don't we take a break? Here." He pulled another energy bar from his pack and handed it to her with a water bottle.

"Are we okay for water?" She accepted it gratefully.

"It's okay, Doc. I'll filter more when we get to the next stream."

"Oh." Marley shifted, brushing away the moisture that sat on her lashes.

"Sit down and rest, while you can." He pointed to a downed tree, and she settled on it.

"Are you going to rest?"

He sat not far from her. "For a minute. I want to

backtrack and check our trail."

Marley felt steadier now that she had something in her stomach. "You think they're still following us?"

"I won't bet against it."

Silence fell between them.

"Zan, what is the plan? I should have asked it earlier, but everything was a bit much, and it was a relief just to lay it on you."

"We're heading for a town. I think I mentioned that. It's about another twelve miles, but I think we can make it there by tonight. Then we'll get some transportation and try to contact General Gallup. They'll make arrangements where to take you, so they can keep you safe while everything is being investigated. Main thing is, they'll be able to stop the immediate distribution of the drug."

Marley felt a chill go down her back.

Zan must've picked it up because he leaned forward placing a hand over hers. "It's going to be all right."

"How? I'm destroying my company. We really are doing a lot of good, but all those men died."

"I doubt your whole company is involved. You weren't, were you?"

Marley realized he had never asked her before. "I did some work in the early phase, but I was kicked off the team." She paused. "That makes me s-sound bitter. But it was-sn't lik-ke that." She took a deep breath to steady the flow of her words. "Sometimes they would pull in others to help run tests, but you really aren't on the team, just extra hands. I haven't had any direct involvement with Gladiator for over a year. Though Dr. Hymas, who's the director over the program asked me yesterday, right after I found the information, if I was interested in taking Dr. Bone's place. Dr. Bone is who sent me the in-nformation, who d-died in the fire last week."

Marley didn't realize she stumbled over the words or gripped Zan's fingers as she was talking. "They killed him, and I think they k-killed the Seavers."

"We'll stop them." He tightened his fingers on hers then released them. "I better check the trail. Wait here."

Marley watched him disappear into the woods, feeling again like the load on her lightened. She really wasn't alone. With Zan helping her, she really could do this.

Two hours later, when she looked at the swollen river, she really wasn't sure she could cross it. They had paralleled the river for almost a mile, and this was their only chance to cross. They had tried to go farther upstream, but there was a cliff blocking their way that Zan decided was too difficult a climb and not worth the risk. So they came back to the tree. Marley wasn't sure it was any less risky. The downed tree was only about four inches around and hung just barely over the current.

As if reading her thoughts, Zan spoke from beside her. "Don't worry. I'll go first and tie off a rope, so you'll have something to hold on to," Zan said with confidence, but Marley could tell the way he stepped up on the log, he was concerned.

There were none of the quick easy movements with which he had crossed the log before. He edged his foot out, testing before he moved his weight on it. He was only about a third of the way across when Marley caught her breath. The log began to sag. Another step and it dipped to only a few inches above the water.

Zan eased forward, and Marley had to fight to keep back a cry as the log shifted. Zan teetered, and, for a second, she thought he'd fall. He caught his balance and steadied himself.

Water lapped over the log, covering the toes of his boots. She knew it had to be slippery under his feet. Still, he moved forward. Marley raised her hand, covering her mouth to keep from crying out and distracting him. What she wanted to do was cover her eyes, but couldn't bring herself to do it.

She reached for him when he wobbled, though a good ten feet separated them. Marley tried to reassure herself if he fell in at least he had the rope tied on him that was attached to the tree behind her. It didn't help much as she pictured him driven into the jagged rocks pushing up through the raging water.

Miraculously, Zan somehow kept his balance. Two more feet and the log got a little wider and no longer dipped into the water. Marley wanted to sigh, but it wasn't over yet. A four-foot long, broken branch jutted almost straight up in the air. It afforded Zan a handhold, but it also meant he had to maneuver around it.

Zan got one foot on the other side when the log shifted again. Zan pitched over. For an instant, it looked like he'd go into the water. He dropped, but somehow, he managed to come down with one knee on the log and gripping the branch, which kept him from going into the river.

"I'm okay," he assured her after a minute, slowly pulling himself up, bringing his other leg around the branch. He stepped out, still keeping his hold on the branch, then releasing it, and took two long strides covering the last of the distance in a leap.

Marley almost dropped to the ground in relief.

"Okay, Marley, it's your turn."

She started to shake her head. "I-I d-don't think I c-can." Her fear made her stuttering come back with a vengeance.

"Yes you can. Look at me, Marley. Yes, you can," he repeated deliberately slow. "I'm going to tie this rope high on this tree, like I did on the one on that side. It will make it so you'll have to reach up above your head for the rope. I want you to take the short piece of rope we used earlier to tether us together while climbing. It's in your jacket pocket. I want you to grab the end and tie it around your waist like I showed you."

"A b-bowline." She concentrated on his words.

"Yes. Can you remember how?"

"I think so." Her hands trembled as she pulled out the rope, but she refused to appear totally helpless in front of him. Wrapping the rope around her waist, then with the end of the rope in her right hand, and her left holding out the other end, she crossed her right hand over, wrapping the rope over her hand.

"Yes, that's it." Zan directed her. "Now pull it down through. Perfect. Now, we're going to tie it over the other rope, but we're going to leave a loop at the top so it will slide over the rope. I'll walk you through it. What we are doing is making a bow-line that is not around you." It took her two tries but she got it.

"Good, now step up on the log then reach up and grab the rope."

"Zan." There was no keeping back the fear.

"You can do it. You can't fall because you're tied on."

Marley closed her eyes trying to block out the raging water, and steady her nerves. She could do this, she thought to herself. When she opened her eyes, she looked directly at Zan. There was confidence in him and anxiousness. She knew if she didn't cross, he would come back for her, and she didn't want that.

She placed a jogging shoe clad foot on the log and, with a deep breath, stepped up.

"That's my girl."

Marley heard the endearment and knew he probably used it on purpose, but she took it to heart. The words warmed her within, and she took a step out onto the log. She wobbled slightly, but with the rope to hang onto, she moved much quicker than he had.

With her lesser weight she was almost halfway across before the log began to dip. Unfortunately, though it remained above the water, it was slippery from Zan's crossing. Marley slowed her pace. Carefully, she placed her foot squarely in the middle and made sure she was steady before shifting the rope.

All the while Zan kept up his encouraging banter and instruction. She was moving smoothly with more confidence when she reached where the branch jutted out. Fortunately, it now tilted off at a ninety degree angle, making it easy to get her lead foot around it. She clung to the rope, letting it take more of her weight, but it remained firm. Slowly, she drew her back leg forward around the branch when the rough bark snagged her shoe lace.

Marley jerked and stumbled. The shoelace came free, but the log shifted again. Marley fought for balance and just regained it when the log dropped from under her feet.

Pain spiked up through her arms. Her outcry was echoed by Zan calling her name.

Chapter Six

Marley clung to the rope dangling over the river. The rope quivered and sagged but held. Marley stared down at the tumultuous water boiling barely beneath her toes.

"Marley, look at me," Zan demanded.

She tore her gaze away from the water. He was at the edge of the bank, leaning out toward her. His arm outstretched but still at least two feet short of reaching her. She glanced back down at the water.

"Look at me," he yelled, pulling her gaze back to him. "You're not going to fall, but I can't reach you." His voice was low, calm, reassuring. "I need you to swing a little closer. Work your legs back and forth. Just like on a swing."

Marley followed him. It took a second to gain any movement. Zan grabbed the rope above him and pulled down so it was lower toward him. As she swung, the line she was holding onto jerked and slid along the rope.

"Good, again. A little closer," Zan directed.

Marley was so focused on her movements and the action on the rope that when Zan caught her around the waist and pulled her into his arms, she cried out, tightening her hold on the rope.

"I have you." He growled the words out against her neck.

Marley felt his hot breath on her fear-chilled skin. Releasing the rope, she sagged down in his arms, her own arms locked around his neck, her toes not even touching the ground.

"I have you," he repeated the words, followed by his lips brushing against her skin.

A shiver ran through her that had nothing to do with her fear of falling but all with the man holding her. He let her slide lower until her feet touched the ground but didn't release her. His hands stroked up and down her back.

Marley went limp, absorbing the feel of him, warm and safe. With her head resting on his chest, she could hear the pounding of his heart. It was a nice beat. She relaxed more, studying the feel of him.

The strap from the pack was rough against her cheek. She wanted to push it away. Instead she shifted her head, rubbing her cheek over an area where just his shirt covered the hard muscle underneath. Marley sighed.

"Hey, are you going to sleep on me." His voice rumbled down to her.

She shook her head, rubbing her cheek against him again in the process. "No, you just feel really good." She gave a little half laugh, feeling happy to be alive and in Zan's arms. Marley really couldn't believe it. She shivered again feeling his hand slide up her back and over her shoulder to cup her cheek, tilting her face up.

His eyes blazed fierce in streaks of cool blue lightening. "You keep saying things like that, and you are going to get yourself into trouble."

"I've never said anything like that before. I usually keep my mouth shut so I don't look stupid, stumbling over my words."

CR80

The thought of her looking stupid took Zan by surprise. The idea was so absurd it made him smile. Her next words shook him more.

"I don't feel awkward talking to you." She looked up at him with such confused earnestness on her face, he knew

76

it was true. Something inside him soared. His breath caught. Unable to stop the motion, he lowered his mouth to hers.

Her lips parted under his gentle pressure, following him into the kiss. He felt the softness of her hair as he buried his fingers in it, holding her head steady for his assault of pleasure. The kiss went on for a full minute before his logic finally forced its way forward enough to remind him of the situation and where they were.

Slowly, he broke the kiss, placing a few smaller brushes of his mouth along her cheek and a last one on her forehead before pulling back. He held her tight a minute more waiting for his breath to steady and giving her time to gain her own composure.

When he stepped back, he looked down, examining her. Her lips were moist, swollen, and a deeper shade of red than normal from his attention. She looked slightly dazed he thought with satisfaction. *Good, because she kept blowing all his sensors.* "You okay?"

She took in a deep breath. "Yes."

"Good. I want to get moving away from the river. Up over that ridge we can stop and get something to eat." He glanced back at the river. "Well, you saved me from having to work the log free and dumping it in the water so no one else can cross it. That should buy us some time and distance before they pick up our trail."

He had Marley sit down and rest while he took two minutes to release the rope, roll it back up and stow it away.

"Ready?" He turned toward her.

Marley nodded.

They were off again, climbing over rocks until the ground evened off. It was a good two mile hike through the valley before they headed up over the next ridge. Luckily, the sky remained clear and the temperature cool, so they made good time. Zan backtracked several times but couldn't see any signs of being followed. For now, they'd lost their pursuers. Crossing the river had gained them some time.

They were deep in the trees when they came upon a small glade.

"Let's take a break," Zan announced, turning in time to see Marley stagger slightly.

"I'm okay," Marley said automatically, straightening her shoulders.

Zan almost smiled at the picture she made. She was exhausted, but still, she hadn't once complained. "Yeah, but we need to keep up our strength," he said, pulling off his pack.

She just collapsed on a rock, sighing in relief. "So what's for dinner?"

"I was thinking Chicken Tetrazzini."

"What?" She laughed.

"Chicken Tetra–" he started to repeat, but she cut him off.

"You're kidding."

"Nope." He tossed her a packet.

She caught it. "What's this?"

"Your tetrazzini."

Her face showed confusion.

"An MRE, that's meals ready to eat. This one's really pretty good, at least, compared to some of the others. Believe me. You don't want to know some of their nicknames."

"Really, what?" She kept looking at him with an openly curious expression.

"Okay, the best one's probably 'four fingers of death'. That's the frankfurters. But the one I really didn't want to eat was the cheese omelet. It is not on our menu. There were times that I chose to starve before I ate it. And I tell you, when you're in a real miserable place, with guns shooting at you, you'd be surprised how good these taste."

As soon as it was out, he wanted to take the last sentence back. He was relieved when Marley changed the subject.

"So what else is on the menu?"

"Tonight, if we don't make it to town, is jambalaya. It's another good one. We have chicken and dumplings for tomorrow. Then things get a little rougher, but we have energy bars to help." He looked down at the food packets he'd been fixing and handed one to her.

"Eat up, Doc."

Marley sighed contently as the food filled her stomach. "Oh, yes." A few minutes later she finished it off with another sigh. "That was good."

"Hey, only the best when I take a lady out." Zan tried to put some mock indignation in his tone. It must have worked because Marley grinned over at him.

"Are you s-saying this is a date?"

"A man's got to take what he gets. This is the closest thing I've had to a date for a while."

"I f-find that hard to b-believe." She grimaced when she stumbled over the words.

"Believe it. I've only been out a couple of months and have been pretty focused on fixing up my house." He didn't add recovering from being shot. Danger was something he didn't want to bring up in this peaceful setting, but Marley broached the subject anyway.

"I'm s-sorry about your house. Do all your dates put your life in jeopardy, get your door broken and windows blown out?"

"Well, you're not boring."

"Actually, I really am."

"No." He cut her off. "Don't ever think that. I said it before and I mean it. I find you beautiful and amazing." His sincerity brought heat into his eyes, and Marley blushed.

She looked down, fiddling with the small packet of crackers from her meal. After a minute, she spoke up.

"How far to town?"

"Five, six miles. It's late but I still think we can make it tonight."

"Then what?"

"I'll see about getting us a car."

She looked horrified. "Steal one?"

"Not unless I have to. That's kind of illegal, and I'd really rather not go to jail in the near future, or distant for that matter."

"Sorry. I th-think this has me a little rattled."

"It's understandable," Zan said easily. "I was thinking more of buying a non-descript clunker if I can find one that runs well."

"I don't think it's safe to go to a bank."

"You're right. No cards either."

"You have enough cash on you?" Shock showed on her face.

She was so easy to read. No wonder the men after her knew she was hiding information. He'd like to get her in a poker game sometime.

"I always keep some for emergencies and I had some extra to pay a couple boys from town that had been helping me clear some wood. They just haven't gotten over for me to pay them yet."

"I'll reimburse you when this is over."

"Don't worry about it."

"That wouldn't be right. I'll never be able to make up for what you've done for me as it is. I can't have you out money besides."

Zan noticed she made it through without stumbling on any words. "I'm thinking we can work something out on the line of you cooking me some gourmet meals." Again he let fire fill his eyes. He knew Marley picked it up because her cheeks colored.

"I-I-I think," she swallowed, "I c-could do that. After a-all, I'll be out of a j-job.

He hated to see her struggle and knew it embarrassed her, but she was so adorable, so flustered. The urge to kiss her again crested over him, but he pushed it away. "Looks like my social life is looking up." When her blush deepened, he stood to keep from reaching for her. "We'd better get going."

They cut over two small hills then met up again with the river, following it. The sound of rushing water masked out all but a few birds and squirrels that let out shrill cries of alarm as they approached. It was beautiful and peaceful then the sound of the water grew to a roar as they rounded the next bend.

"Oh, wow." Marley exclaimed as they reached where the water dropped twenty to thirty feet. A rainbow slashed across the mist. "It's beautiful." She breathed in deeply, taking pleasure in the sight.

Zan smiled back at her, pausing about six feet in front of her. "You like waterfalls?"

"Oh, yes. Love them. There is just something about them." She let it hang.

"I agree. There's a couple north of here that I will have to take you to sometime."

Marley was surprised how easy the comment came from him. As if he already put them together in the future in some kind of permanent basis. She tried to tell herself she was reading more into it but couldn't hold back the rush of emotion that flowed through her. She was falling in love with Zan.

It didn't matter that she'd only known him two days, well not even a full two days. He'd slid into a place in her heart that no man had ever touched. "I'd like–"

The sharp crack of a gunshot echoed through the canyon, cutting her off.

Zan jerked, spun to the side then dropped over the edge of the embankment. One instant he was there, the next he was gone.

Chapter Seven

Marley screamed Zan's name, unable to take her eyes off the place he'd been a full second before she could accept the reality of what happened. She rushed to the edge, afraid she'd see his body broken on the rocks below, but he wasn't there.

Her panic didn't lessen when she caught sight of him a good thirty yards downstream. Zan bobbed in the current. He was face up but appeared to be unconscious. She prayed he was just unconscious.

Marley took off running just as another shot rang out, kicking up dust where she'd been. Not breaking her stride, she ducked low and glanced across the valley. She caught a glimpse of the familiar red and white security vehicle before the trees cut off the view.

Her attention darted to the small rough trail that ran along the edge of the embankment then back to Zan. She was gaining on him, but the current still carried him along. His body bounced off a rock, and Marley could've sworn he reacted.

She refused to accept that it was wishful thinking and ran harder, paying more attention to the trail. She had to get far enough in front of him to be able to climb down and catch him as he floated by. She just hoped she could get to him before he sank and drowned.

Marley leapt over rocks and exposed roots, moving at breakneck speed. She glanced at the water and realized she was at least twenty feet ahead of Zan. The bank had dropped to only about six feet above the waterline. Still she'd need more space to get over the rocks to have a chance of reaching him.

Bushes jutted out before her as she rounded a bend. Marley ducked under the branches, her arm up in front of her face, and forced herself to continue through, heedless of the limbs whipping at her. She broke out of the foliage and made a four foot leap to a sandbar, where the river started to spread out and become shallow.

She skidded to a stop and turned just in time to see Zan round the bend. Wading out in the water, she was about hip deep when she got into location and planted her feet. Still, the impact of his body took her down.

Marley locked one arm around him and rolled with him coming back to the surface. She forced her legs down beneath her. Rocks tumbled out from under her feet, and she was pulled downstream. Marley fought to angle their way to the side.

They were at the end of the sandbar by the time the water only reached her knees, and she got Zan beached. Marley sucked in air as she pulled several more times, dragging him by the straps of his backpack. Water lapped at his feet when she decided it was good enough and dropped down.

Blood trickled down the side of his head, but she ignored it, reaching for his neck to check for a pulse. She almost collapsed with relief when she realized he was breathing. It was the sight of a blood stain blossoming on the upper shoulder of his shirt, radiating out from under his backpack strap that spurred her forward next.

"Zan." His name escaped her lips.

It took her a second to release the buckle on his pack and move the strap out of the way to reveal the tattered edges of the hole in his shirt marking the inside bloody ring. Marley fought to stay calm. Since his clothes were too soaked to just feel for dampness, she worked her hand over Zan's shoulder, feeling for the damage on his back. When her tentative probe brought no signs, she laid her hand flat to cover more area. Her finger traced a roughened area, but she knew whatever it was it had healed.

"No exit wound," she said to herself.

That meant the bullet was still in him. *You can do this. First we need to get the backpack off and control the bleeding.*

She was just as wet as he was so didn't have anything dry to use to pack the wound. Her attention went to the backpack. Zan had pulled an amazing amount of gear out of it. It had to have a first aid kit.

Untying his jacket from around her waist, she laid it out then released the buckle around his waist and the other shoulder. She eased him over onto the raincoat. Her fingers shook slightly as she went to work on his buttons. Easing the shirt apart, she faced his dull green T-shirt.

Marley reached for the large knife in the sheath on his backpack strap. It stuck at her first attempt but when she tugged, it pulled free. She froze at the sight of a hole bored out halfway up the blade. It lined up with the hole in his shoulder, and she knew the bullet had gone through it. She paused a second before removing the knife strapped to his leg. The wicked looking blade made her shiver, but it sliced effortlessly through the T-shirt material.

Marley was more jarred by the large scar that puckered Zan's skin several inches below where blood seeped around the dime sized hole. She tore her attention away knowing she had to hurry. Her mind skidded over the anatomy of the shoulder and felt a touch of clinical relief.

As long as it wasn't any deeper than it appeared, and she got the bleeding stopped, and Zan didn't get an infection, the wound shouldn't be too serious. Muscles and tissue but nothing life threatening, still, it would be painful, and Marley knew it would be easiest on him to tend it while he was unconscious.

The first aid kit was in the third pocket she checked and amazingly everything in the pack seemed dry. More amazing was what was in the kit. Pressure bandages, suture kit, antibiotics and pain medication. It was serious medical supplies, not the wimpy normal first aid kit stuff.

Marley was also surprised her hands no longer shook as she laid everything out. Step by step she ran through everything needed in her mind. She cleaned her hands and pulled on a pair of rubber gloves. Cleansed around the wound with sterile pads, then she swabbed the area with iodine soaked swabs from another packet. With one more steadying breath, she went to work with a scalpel and tweezers she'd removed from a sterile packet.

She was relieved when she found the bullet barely below the surface and it seemed intact though smashed out. The knife had saved him from most of the damage. She checked the wound thoroughly before cleaning it out. Marley held her breath hoping Zan wouldn't wake with the pain. Mercifully, he remained unconscious.

A few minutes later, Marley finished bandaging the wound and sat back sighing in relief. Because of her field of study, her rotations at the hospital had only been cursory, but it was surprising how easy it was to slip back into the persona.

Checking his pulse one more time, she shifted her attention to his head, cleaning the inch long cut at the edge of his hairline. Instead of stitching the wound, Marley elected to seal it with the medical glue she found. That finished, she roamed her hands over his body until she was satisfied he had no other injuries.

Marley sat back and looked down at the man who had come to mean so much to her. The clinical demeanor that had kept her together faded, and tears streaked down her face.

"Zan," she brushed his cheek with her finger, wishing

he would wake up, relieved that he didn't because of the pain he'd be in. "I'm so sorry."

She wanted to run. Get as far away from him as possible, so he would be safe. She even thought of turning herself in and letting them kill her but knew that wouldn't work. They knew he'd helped her. They would never let him live because of what she might have told him. And, with his connection to the military, he could get people to listen, at least enough to open an investigation.

Marley held back the scream that wanted to escape. She still had things to do. She needed to make Zan safe. They needed a place to hide. They were too exposed with him lying out on the sandbar if the helicopter flew over. She also needed to get him dry and keep him warm.

Leaving him was hard, but it only took her a couple minutes to find a place about a hundred feet away that was tucked between a couple boulders and sheltered by some massive trees. The only question was how she was going to get him there. Marley decided to move the pack first and take a minute to lay out the sleeping bag before returning for Zan.

Knowing there was no way she could carry him, she used his raincoat as a travois to drag him on. Getting him over the small shallow stream and up on the bank was tricky. Marley was exhausted by the time she had him clear of the water.

She sank down beside him to catch her breath and check his vitals before continuing. It took her two more stops before she got him to the camp and faced the next dilemma, getting him out of his wet clothes.

It was funny. She was a doctor and knew the human body inside and out, but the thought of stripping Zan down made her pause. It told her just how much he meant to her. She didn't see him as just a man. He was Zan. Someone she cared for. Someone she was interested in.

"He's just a man. A human body." Saying the words

aloud didn't help much, but she went to work.

Since she'd already opened the shirt when tending the wound, she was able to ease it down and off, then worked it from under his body. The T-shirt was easier. Not worried about saving it, since she'd already pretty much ruined it, she just cut the rest of it away.

Marley shifted to his feet removing his boots and socks. For a second, she was caught at the size and corded ridges of them. She shoved the thought away and reached for his belt.

"You are a doctor," she repeated but looked away as she slid his pants down his muscled legs, letting her attention fix on several other scars. The moment she got his pants clear, she went to work shifting him into the sleeping bag and getting him covered up. That done, she dropped limply down beside him.

Marley rested several minutes before the need to finish preparing the camp pressed her back into action. First, she went back to the sandbar to make sure she hadn't left anything and washed Zan's shirt the best she could. On her way back to the hiding place, she brushed out their trail the way she'd seen Zan do.

Marley then used Zan's damaged knife to cut some bushes, jabbing them into the mud to block the trail they'd used. Once she'd done everything she could think of to hide their trail, she worked her way back to camp, following the process with the bushes twice more.

Back at camp, Marley checked Zan one more time then decided to go through his pack to see what she might use. She had just started when the sound of voices reached her. Marley froze, wanting to believe she'd imagined the sound.

A minute went by. She was about to relax when the voices reached her again, this time closer.

"I can't make it down there. You go down and check it out."

"What? That little wash?"

Marley felt fear as she recognized the voice of Drew Jansen, the security guard from the lab.

"Yeah."

"You can't think she's down there. You saw her jack rabbit just like she did before. She's long gone, at least the dude's out of the way."

They were close enough, she could hear Jansen's wheeze.

"You should've shot her instead," Mills, the security chief, snapped.

"I told you, I couldn't get the shot."

"Well, you'd better get down there and make sure she's not there. We have to be the ones to find her or there could be some uncomfortable questions raised. Hymas is already spitting mad about her getting away."

Marley realized they were on the embankment almost directly above her. She looked up. The slight overhang and trees kept them from her view. She just hoped it would be the same if they looked down.

A dusting of dirt trickled down from the edge. Marley leaned over Zan to keep it from landing on him. She couldn't risk him waking now. Thankfully, he remained unconscious.

"With him out of the way, she'll be easy to find. It was just rotten luck she stumbled into him." Jansen's voice reached down to her.

"So you say. I still think she could've been seeing him. Now get down there."

"I'm going. And I told you, I've been keeping an eye on her for a while. She's not been seeing anyone." Jansen's voice faded, but Marley didn't dare move though a wave of sickness ran through her at the thought that he'd been watching her.

A minute later, she heard branches break as he moved through. Marley followed his progress along the river. When he came close to the trail where she'd dragged Zan along, she reached for the dart gun she'd laid out. She cradled it in her lap and hoped she could figure out how to fire it, but the crashing continued on.

She wondered if there wasn't something else she should've done. Had she missed something? Would Jansen, with the ever-present crude sneer, just stumble onto them? She jumped when his shout broke the silence.

"You can't get through this way. I told you, she rabbited. I'm betting she went over the hill toward the road. And the way she runs, she's probably three miles from here by now." His wheezing was more pronounced.

Marley heard the thrashing through the trees grow louder again, but instead of coming closer to the hiding place, Jansen stayed down by the river, moving at a quicker pace.

"Let's head back to the truck," Mills answered back, his voice coming from a ways off. "We need to get into position if anyone finds a body and starts to wonder so they don't tie it to us."

For a full five minutes, Marley didn't dare do anything but breathe, and even that seemed labored as fear flowed over her. They'd been so close. Her fingers were still shaking when she put the gun down.

Dropping her head to her hands, she fought to calm her fear. They were gone. They hadn't found them. She let the thoughts echo in her mind. She'd kept Zan safe, but there was still more to be done. She just wished she could stop shaking. Locking onto the thought, her mind finally processed that she was cold. The knowledge spurred her into action.

Digging through the backpack she wasn't surprised to find a change of clothes for Zan in a sealed bag. With only a second's hesitation, Marley stripped out of her wet clothes and pulled on his dry shirt. Even with his belt cinched up his pants bagged on her, but she was warm.

Marley laid out their clothes to dry then followed the

directions and made up her own MRE, this time chicken and dumplings. She found it passably good. With the dart gun in her lap, she settled down next to Zan to keep watch as the sun set.

Marley jerked awake. It took several seconds for her eyes to adjust to the darkness and reality to slip back in.

Fear crept in with it.

She listened. Afraid to breathe, but the only noise that reached her ears were the sounds of frogs, cicadas and the chorus of other night bugs, and she relaxed.

A shifting on the ground by her feet made her jump, and she knew what had disturbed her.

"Zan." She turned, barely able to make him out in the moonlight breaking through the cloudy sky.

Marley crawled to him. Reaching out a hand, she lay it on his forehead barely getting time to determine there was no fever when the blow caught her. She never saw it coming. One moment she was on her knees, the next thrown back three feet. Pain sliced through her side even though she knew it was a glancing contact.

Zan continue to thrash as she gulped in air to replace what had been knocked from her. After a minute, Marley righted herself and reached for him again, instinctively trying to keep him from hurting himself. She pulled back at the last instant to miss another strike that would have likely broken her nose.

"Zan, Zan, it's Marley. It's Marley," she repeated his name and her name until he began to still. "It's all right." She touched her fingers to his arm, ready to dodge.

He jerked, but as she said his name again, he relaxed.

"It's all right." She ran her hand up and down his arm, caressing his brow with her other hand. His breathing became more even.

"Zan, do you know who I am?"

"My Marley."

Her name sounded like it was drawn out over rough

gravel but never better. She was shocked and pleased at the possessiveness of the tone. "Yes." She stroked her hand down his cheek, a smile coming to her lips.

She had thought he'd gone back to sleep when he spoke, clearer this time. "What happened?"

"Here drink this." She reached for the water she'd left beside him and raised his head up a little to take a couple swallows. "Not too much. We don't want you to get sick."

He took a second swallow and sighed. He seemed more alert. As if to prove the point, he repeated the question. "What happened?" This time, his voice was much stronger, and he shifted, trying to sit up.

"No, stay down. You were shot. I got the bullet out. It didn't do too much damage, but your body's had a shock. You fell into the water and hit your head at some time."

"You took the bullet out?" He locked on the first thing she said.

"Yes, it wasn't deep, fortunately. It was just tissue and a little muscle damage. It went through your knife in your backpack strap."

He nodded and grimaced.

"Easy, do you need some more pain medicine?"

"No. How long have I been out?"

"About f-four hours."

He pulled up. "Where are we?"

"A couple hundred yards down r-river, I'd guess. I'm not sure how far you f-floated from where we were."

"You got me out?"

"Yes."

"And here?"

She couldn't find the words to answer because the image of him bleeding on the bank was too clear, along with the sound of the men moving above them. His hand came out of the darkness to catch her arm.

"Marley?"

She couldn't believe she felt steadier just having him

touch her. "You drifted q-quite a ways before I could get ahead of you and down the bank. I was afraid you'd drown. Mills and Jansen, the lab's security, showed up. It was Jansen who shot you. I'd covered our trail l-like you had."

ᏣᎦᏋᏗ

"Marley," he said her name again, sliding his hand down to take hers. "You're cold."

"I'm fine. We sh-should get you something to eat if you feel up to it."

"I could eat." Zan caught a good look at Marley as his small light flared to life. She was dressed in his clothes. Her hair was a wild mass around her head. It made him realize he didn't have a comb in his pack. It wasn't something he worried about with his hair so short.

She looked untamed, an all-natural woman. He wondered what she'd think of that. He figured that was not an image she'd ever apply to herself but he liked it. Then again he figured she would deny how incredible she did on rescuing and taking care of him. She'd taken out a bullet.

He shifted his arm and felt a stab of pain, but he could handle it.

"Here." She was back beside him. "Just Ibuprofen."

She dropped four in his hand and waited for him to take them. Zan did so without any complaint. She turned back to get the food, and he started to shift up. Pain ripped through his shoulder. A faint hiss escaped his lips before he could stop it.

Marley spun back, reaching for him. "Let me help."

He felt her soft hands against his skin and realized he didn't have his shirt on. Of course, for her to tend him, she'd have to have taken it off. Cut it off. He grimaced with the thought.

As he shifted he also came to the fact he didn't have his pants on. It made sense, if he went into the river he'd be soaked. Still, he was almost shocked his timid little Marley had managed that.

He wondered what she thought of his body then flinched, thinking of the assortment of scars he carried. He'd lived a tough life and had the marks to prove it though he was still in good physical condition.

Her hand slid over his skin, and he took a deep breath, catching the gentle scent that was all Marley.

"Easy." She sounded almost breathless as she shifted his pack behind him to lean against.

He looked up to meet her eyes and could've sworn she was blushing, but the tint of the glow made it impossible to tell. On impulse, he reached up and brushed back her hair with his good hand. "You did good, Doc."

Her shoulders dipped almost imperceptibly and her eyes closed. When she opened them again, she gave him a weak smile. He could make out moisture in the corners.

"Thanks," she whispered. "I thought I'd lost you." Her voice wobbled, but there was no stuttering. "Don't ever do that to me again," she added forcefully at the end.

"Yes, ma'am," he shot back and a smile cracked her lips. "You said something about food, or was that just to taunt me?"

She held the food while he ate. He felt better when he'd finished, though fatigue slipped back over his body.

"Lay back down now," she said, as she eased him up to remove the pack from behind him. She settled him back to the ground, and pulled the sleeping bag up, tucking him in.

He caught her arm as she started to move away. He didn't speak until she looked at him. "You need rest, too."

"I am."

He was already shaking his head. "Get the gun and come lay over here."

"I'm fine. I have your clothes."

"They're not enough. You're still cold."

"I'm—"

"Don't argue. You want me to sleep, you come lay here."

"You don't…" This time she broke off on her own, but he knew what she was going to say.

"But you do." He tried but couldn't hold back the comment. "And how did I get my clothes off?"

She bristled, but this time Zan knew for sure she was blushing.

"There was no choice, and I am a doctor. I even did a rotation in a hospital."

"Get the gun, Marley, and come lay down."

She waited a full minute before complying. Timidly, she stretched out beside the sleeping bag, close enough to receive some warmth, but he wasn't satisfied.

"Place the gun on the ground above our heads."

The instant she released it, he reached out his good arm pulling her inside the bag. Pain spiked. He tried to ignore it but lost his hold.

"Stop. You'll hurt yourself." She rolled over him, her hand going to his shoulder, running over his skin an inch above the bandage.

"Then settle down." He sighed with relief when she eased her feet inside the bag and snuggled down along his side. The bag was tight, not made for two. He knew she wasn't covered all the way, but at least she would be warmer.

cs80

The next thing Zan knew, the sun was just spearing rays of light over the mountains. Pain sliced through his shoulder. He pushed it back, compartmentalizing it like he'd learn to do years earlier. Instead, he focused on the small hand that rested squarely on the center of his chest. He could feel each fingertip and the heat that radiated from them. The heat matched and melded into the warmth that ran along his side where Marley lay snuggled.

Her breath tickled a line across his chest. Looking down, he could just see the mahogany crown of her head. Carefully, he bent his elbow, raising his right hand to run his fingers through the fine strands. Light caught the locks and they burned with radiance. Zan marveled at the color and feel. He never knew anything could be so soft and beautiful.

Becoming conscious of the slight chill still in the air, he eased the sleeping bag higher on her shoulder. He was rewarded with the slight stroking of her fingers on his chest. He remained still, letting his eyes close, absorbing the pleasure, tempted to return to sleep. He knew they should get going, but when Marley shifted, aligning along him, Zan gave in to the simple pleasure of her and the need for more rest. He drifted back to sleep, snug and warm, with Marley at his side, where he could dream of her there forever.

❧

The sound of a squirrel chattering in the tree overhead brought Marley awake. She became aware of the chill in the air on one of her cheeks, but the rest of her was heavenly warm. She basked in it until the memory of Zan being shot filtered back to her. She started to move, but the arm along her back held her in place.

"No, just a minute more." Zan's voice was gravelly, but she detected no hint of pain.

"Zan?" she said his name as his hand made delicious, little stroking motions on her back.

"Yes."

"How are you?"

"I'm holding you, I'm perfect." After a second, he continued. "I could handle waking up like this forever."

"You got shot."

"Okay, we can skip that part. You did a good job tending it, Doc."

Marley thought she felt him press a kiss into her hair. "You haven't seen it yet."

"I can tell."

"Are you in much pain?"

"Nothing I can't handle."

"I should get you more pain medication." She couldn't bring herself to pull away.

"Just Ibuprofen, I need to be alert."

Marley started to protest, but when she raised her head, his lips brushed her forehead.

"It's okay," he growled out. "I can handle it. I've had worse."

Her mind went to the scar on his shoulder just below where he was shot. It would have been dangerously close to his heart. She traced her fingers over the edges of it. "What happened to your shoulder?" She wasn't sure he'd answer, but his reply came easily.

"I got shot about six months ago. We were jumping into a spot that I can't admit to." There was almost a touch of humor in his voice. "We weren't as stealthy as we were supposed to be. Actually, it just so happened a guard looked up at an inopportune time. Getting me out was a little rough, but my guys completed the mission and did it."

He fell silent. Marley knew what he was saying. He owed his men, and they were in danger because of the Gladiator drug.

"I never asked what you were in the military."

"Army Ranger." He released her abruptly. "We need to get going."

Marley turned, practically rolling over him, pinning him down with surprise. "Not until I check your wound." She gave him her sternest look.

He lay still in obvious shock then a smile crested on his lips.

"You're beautiful, Doc." His right hand slid up her back, spearing into her hair. Before she could stop him or even think, his hand clamped on her neck, urging her head down until their lips met. He kissed her deeply, drawing her out, savoring her.

Marley returned it with pleasure. Her hand coming up

to caress his stubble roughened cheek. Nothing had ever been so intriguing or right.

When the pressure eased, she drew back several inches, looking down into his eyes. Heat burned there for her to see.

"Good morning, Doc."

His words rumbled through her heart. He was right. She could get used to waking up like this.

Chapter Eight

Marley scooted out of the sleeping bag, her face warmed from his kiss and the thought that she'd actually slept there beside him. She'd never done anything like that before, especially kissing him that way. She couldn't get her mind off it. Ignoring the satisfied look on his face, she got him the Ibuprofen and checked his shoulder, pleased at how it looked.

Marley hurried to her clothes. Fortunately, they were mostly dry. She snatched them up and went behind the tree to change. She knew her actions were silly as she folded his clothes into a neat pile, but she had to have something to do while she fought to calm her racing heart.

It was one thing to know she'd fallen in love with Zan, now she was thinking of forever. She tried to convince herself that it was because he'd said the word first. He wasn't serious. He couldn't be. They'd known each other two days, and guys just didn't think that way. She was just being her foolish, nerdy self.

Drawing in a deep breath, she let it out slowly. Steadying herself, she walked back around the tree. Her gaze immediately went to Zan, and all her efforts for calm shattered. Forever came right back to her mind, and she wanted it more than she'd ever wanted anything else.

"H-here." She laid the clothes beside him. "You'll n-need these. I-I'll be in the trees." She turned and fled.

CustO

Zan knew he flustered her but, with the heat blooming on her face, he couldn't feel remorse. Marley was such a sweet package, a gift just for him. One he planned to treasure for the rest of his life.

That brought him pause. He'd have to be more careful to make sure they had a long life together. And that meant, get moving.

Pain stabbed as he sat up. He raised his hand to rest it over the bandage. Another scar and another too close call, but Marley had done a terrific job tending it. She was amazing, whether she knew it or not. It was just one more thing he wanted to teach her.

It took effort pulling on his pants, but he managed them. He halted at his shirt.

"Marley."

"Yes," she answered from not far off.

"I need help with my shirt."

A second later, she appeared through the bushes. She looked more composed. She'd tried to tame her wild hair by tying a piece of cord around it to hold it back, but without a comb or brush, it still had a hint of disarray.

She walked to him, taking the shirt from his hand. Her eyes flickered over the skin of his chest. He picked up the telltale sign of heat on her cheeks, satisfied she liked what she saw.

Marley eased his shirt up his injured arm, then held it out and helped guide his other arm in, accomplishing it with hardly any pain.

"One more thing, could you help with the socks and boots, too." He gave her an innocent look that she returned with a smile.

The tension eased from her.

After a quick breakfast, they stowed their gear. When he went to reach for the pack, she stopped him.

"No, I'll carry it."

The objection was on his lips but he conceded.

Nodding, instead he picked up the knife that had been in the strap sheath. He turned it over studying the punctured blade.

It truly had saved him. Maybe not his life, but from an injury that would have kept him from being able to keep them safe. He took a rock and with a couple carefully placed blows tamped down the jagged edges then worked it back into its sheath.

"It still might come in handy."

Marley struggled getting the pack into place but it took a hand from Zan to settle and adjust the straps until it rested comfortably.

"Ready?" she asked with gusto.

"Lead the way."

She led through the bushes to the river.

"Nice job." He studied her camouflage efforts. "You learn fast."

"That's what they always said." She paused. "I'm not quite sure where we are."

He laughed. He couldn't help it. It just rolled out of him as he pulled out his GPS.

They paced their hike much slower than the day before, with frequent breaks for rest and to give Marley time to check his wound, which she insisted on doing regularly. It was late afternoon when Zan lead them through the trees where it opened into a park in a residential section of town.

Since there were hiking trails off the park, Zan wasn't too concerned about causing a disturbance as they walked through the neighborhood. He did insist on taking the backpack, though, because it would draw attention if she was carrying one and he wasn't. Slinging it on just his good shoulder, they walked casually along as if deep in conversation after an ordinary day on the trail.

They'd only gone a block and a half when Zan stopped. "I think we're in luck."

"What?" Marley looked around.

He nodded across the street and down the block. A white and blue motorcycle rested on the lawn.

"The motorcycle?" Doubt filled her voice. She couldn't keep it back.

"It's all right, Marley. Just let me go check it out first. Why don't you take the backpack and go wait back at the park out of sight?"

There was hesitancy in her but she nodded, taking over the backpack.

Zan caught her hand, pulling her around to him. "I won't be long. Just stay out of sight until I get there." He leaned down and kissed her, one swift kiss.

Zan watched her make it most of the way back to the park before he headed across the street and up the sidewalk to the door. He rang the bell. The door was opened by a middle-aged woman a few seconds later.

"Hello, ma'am. I saw the motorcycle on your lawn and was wondering about it."

"Oh." The woman picked up a pleased look. "It's my son's. Just a minute, if you don't mind." She motioned to the lawn.

"Not at all." Zan stepped down as she closed the door.

Behind him, he heard her call, "Dennis, there's someone to look at your bike."

Zan walked over and looked at the machine. It looked in pretty good shape. It was a little old. The price on the sign was reasonable, especially if it ran well.

He crouched down looking over the tires and ran his hand over the forks making sure they weren't bent.

"Hi," a young man called as he bounded off the porch.

Zan stood and turned to greet him. "Hi." Doing a quick survey, he figured the boy was about eighteen or nineteen. His hair was slightly long but otherwise he looked pretty clean-cut. Zan reached out his hand, and the young man took it easily, giving it a shake.

"My girlfriend and I have been up hiking and I noticed your bike. How's it run?" Zan nodded to the bike.

"Real good. I've done a lot of the work on it myself. Put in a new clutch about two months ago."

"You any good with machines?" Zan looked over at him.

"Yes, sir." The boy straightened, puffing out his chest a little. It was funny that even though he was out of the military, young men still seemed to address him as sir.

"Why don't you start it up, so we can have a listen?"

"Sure." Dennis straddled the motorcycle and started it. The engine kicked right over and settled into a nice smooth sound. Several times, Dennis revved it up then let it idle back. He watched, and when Zan nodded, switched it off. "Do you like it?" There was no missing the hopeful tone in the young man's voice.

"Yes. It reminds me of one I used to have when I was about your age." *About a million years ago.* "So, why you selling it?"

"I'm going to school up north and need a car more than a bike." There was also no missing Dennis wished he could keep the motorcycle but was resigned to what needed to be done.

"Is the tank full?"

"Not quite, but I have a jug in the garage. I can top it off."

"Good. Do you happen to have two helmets you could sell with it?"

"Yes, sir. I'll be right back." He ran to the garage and reappeared a second later with two real decent, full-face helmets.

Zan nodded. "One last thing, how about a leather jacket?"

This time, Dennis looked puzzled, then thoughtful. "I have one, but there's no way it would fit you."

It was Zan's turn to laugh. "I suspect your right. I want

it for my girlfriend until I know for sure if she likes riding or not. Would you be willing to sell it for an extra, say, hundred and fifty for jacket and the helmets?"

"Oh yeah, sure. The jacket's old and a little beat up, but it's clean," he said honestly.

Zan knew Dennis was afraid he'd take back the offer. "Sounds good. Why don't you get me the gas can, and I'll fill it up while you grab the jacket, title, and a paper, so we can write up a bill of sale?"

"Yeah, sure." The young man brightened.

Five minutes later, Zan straddled the motorcycle, and it roared to life. The motor sounded real good. He figured the kid really was a pretty fair mechanic. Again, he reminded him of himself. Zan touched his fingers to his helmet as he pulled away. Dennis waved back, the money clutched tight in his hand.

For a moment, Zan was tempted to goose the motorcycle into a wheelie but decided that his shoulder, though less painful than it probably had a right to be, was in no condition to do the stunt.

When he pulled into the park and saw no sign of Marley, he was proud of how well she'd followed his directions, but when she didn't immediately appear, he felt a stab of fear. A second later, she moved from the shadow of the trees to the right of him. Zan drove over to meet her.

"You bought it."

He heard the underlying trepidation in her words. "Yes, it will be easier for us to move around." It was then he realized she'd probably never been on a motorcycle before.

He swung his leg over the bike and stepped toward her. "Don't worry, Marley. I'll teach you. Trust me?" He extended his hand.

There was no hesitation in her nod or her reaching out her hand to his. "What about your shoulder?" she asked in concern.

"It'll be all right. I'll mainly only need it for working the clutch. Now we need to disguise you a little until we can get you some different clothes. So let's put your jacket in here, and you wear this." He held out the kid's worn leather jacket.

Marley slipped it on. The fit was good, better than he'd hoped. "Good. Now can you pull up your hair so it doesn't show under the helmet?"

She held her ponytail on top of her head while he helped work the helmet on. "That'll work. You'll have to carry the backpack. There's no way I can carry it with you on back."

He removed the sheath from the strap and placed it and the knife inside. "That's better. Packs are common enough that, hopefully, it won't give us away."

"Give us away?"

"If anyone's searching, they might have a description of us out. I'm not wearing my fatigues, so that helps. But until we can put some more distance between us and here, I'd rather keep it so they don't link us with a motorcycle."

"They think you're dead."

He picked up her shiver and reached out, giving her hand a squeeze. "That's also to our advantage."

"So what do we do?"

"Avoid security cameras like those around banks that might pick us up. There's a shopping area on the east side of town. We'll head there. Park about a block away. Then I'll go buy a disposable phone, while you go into the clothing store and buy yourself a pair of jeans, a couple shirts, and whatever else you need for a several days. Nothing flashy that'll stand out. " He turned and swung his leg back over the bike, then looked back to her waiting.

"I-I thought you were going to t-teach me?"

"I am, come on."

Cautiously, she stepped forward, swinging her leg over like she'd seen him do, settling on the seat behind him.

"Good. Now these are your foot-pegs. Keep your feet on them at all times. Don't worry, I'll balance us. Whatever you do, don't put your feet down and don't touch this."

"The exhaust pipe."

"Very good, Doc. Yes, it will burn you."

"I understand."

"Good. Wrap your arms around my waist. Just relax your body and let it follow mine." He reached back, tipped down her face shield then his own, and started the engine.

Marley clamped her arms around him then tightened down in a death grip as they started to move. After several blocks, she eased a little. Still, he was conscious of every curve of her pressed along his back.

Zan kept their route to the neighborhoods avoiding the main section of town. As he said, he stopped a block from the shopping center in the end parking space of a fitness club.

"How'd you do?" he asked Marley as he turned to her.

Her face sparked with excitement. "It's kind of fun."

He smiled. "It gets better. I'll teach you to drive it when this is over."

"Deal."

"I'm turning you into a wild woman."

She just grinned back happily, and for a moment, the danger was forgotten. Unfortunately, it came right back.

"We'll leave the helmets, leather jacket and backpack here."

"You're not worried about someone stealing them?"

"I'll hide them back in the bushes." He pulled out his wallet and handed her some money. "You head over to the store. It's just around the corner on your left. I'll wait five minutes and cross to the store over there. We'll meet here in a half-hour. Leave on the clothes you have on now until you get back here."

"Okay."

"Wait a minute." He reached out and pulled the

ponytail holder from her hair, fluffing it out around her shoulders.

"Now that's a mess."

"Just adding to the wild image."

She shook her head. "I'll never get a brush through it." She drew in a deep breath.

"Just relax and act natural. You're just going shopping."

"I'm not a great shopper."

"That's nice to know." He tilted his head in the direction of the store.

෬෫

Marley felt strange walking into the store. Though she'd never been there before, it was one of the chains she most often shopped at. The familiarity of it was shocking after the events of the last few days. She was tempted to look back and see if she could catch a glimpse of Zan but held in the impulse. Grabbing a cart, she made her way to the jeans section.

Zan hadn't said anything about being cautious with money, but she knew what he had on him was all they had, and they couldn't risk using credit cards or ATMs to get cash. She thumbed through the jeans quickly, avoiding the more expensive ones. She selected seven pair to try on.

Conscious of the fact that she wanted to look good for Zan, she paused, her hand hovering above the shirt she was about to pick up. Funny, she'd never bought clothes with a man in mind before. She ended up grabbing up nine tops before heading for the dressing room.

Marley flinched at the sight of herself in the mirror. Her clothes were wrinkled and had patches of dirt. She definitely looked wild with her mass of hair in such disarray. But, there was also a different change in her, a spark she'd never seen before. She wondered if love really did show on someone. Pushing the thought away, she hurried to try on the clothes.

Quickly she went through the jeans until she had it narrowed down to just two pair. She shifted to the shirts, ending up with a three-quarter-length sleeve, mid-weight sweater, and a scoop-neck t-shirt. Her attention went back to the pants, trying them each on again, checking the fit. Marley decided on the one that hugged her nicely but wasn't too tight that it would be uncomfortable sitting on the motorcycle. She took her selections, stopping to add underwear, and a dark blue T-shirt for Zan on the way to the check out.

She walked out of the store twenty-six minutes after she entered it. Zan wasn't at the bike when she got there. She'd just retrieved the pack when he showed up.

"I thought we could use some food." He held up a sack from the fast food place on the corner.

"Oh, yes." She groaned with anticipation.

"A weakness Doc?"

"If you have French fries in there, yes."

"Why Doc, they aren't good for you," he mocked her lightly.

"But they are so good."

He reached into the bag and held up a French fry. She snatched the bag instead.

"Hey." He stuffed the fry in his mouth then took the hamburger she held out for him and settled down on the grass next to her.

"Were you able to get a phone?" she asked after taking several bites to satisfy her hunger.

"Yes, I tried to get through to General Gallup but I'm afraid it's too late. I stressed it was an emergency, but he's off base and cannot be contacted. We'll have to wait until morning and try back."

As if not giving her time for disappointment to set in, he continued. "I also got some snacks and something for you." He reached in the shopping bag and pulled out a brush.

Marley couldn't keep back the smile, touched at the thought. "Thank you."

"You're welcome. As soon as you finish eating, why don't you slip behind that shed and change clothes. Nobody will be able to see you, and I'll stand watch."

Marley wanted to protest. She'd never done anything like changing outside where people were around before, but Zan was right, it was private. Still, she made it through in record time.

Feeling slightly embarrassed, she came out brushing her hair. It took her a second to realize Zan was staring at her. She froze.

"Is something wrong? Did I miss a tag?" She looked down then shifted to look behind her.

He groaned. "I swear your legs look a mile long. You do great things for jeans."

Shocked, Marley jerked her head up to find herself wrapped in the heat of his appraisal. "Y-you like?"

"Oh yeah." He walked toward her, his eyes never leaving her. "But, I like what's inside more," he growled the words out right before his head swooped down to capture her lips with his. His arms locked around her, hauling her up tight against him. The kiss continued until the blast of a horn pulled them apart.

Marley steadied herself with a hand on his chest. "Oh." She looked up to find him watching her. The planes of his face were harsh, but she felt no fear. "You know, I've been kissed more in two days than I have my entire life. I like it."

"We'll have to see we continue that." There was no teasing smile, just the gleam of promise.

Chapter Nine

For two hours Zan had been aware of every inch of Marley lined along his body. Her delicate hands pressed to his stomach. Even when she leaned back to look around, he was aware of her there. It was just as it had been with his shirt all morning as they hiked, her scent lingered on it, drifting up to fill his senses.

It still almost surprised him how easily Marley had taken to riding. She had given her trust over to him as she had done on everything else, following his instructions and lead. He wanted to pass it off that Marley was the most trusting person ever, but he knew that wasn't true.

Marley had thick walls around her heart. She'd had to over the years to withstand the pressures she'd been put under and survive as emotionally intact as she was. Marley guarded her inner self well. But for some reason, she had opened up, letting him in.

Zan vowed to cherish the gift as he would always cherish her. Fire from the declaration burned within him. He tried to tell himself that it was too soon to be having thoughts like that, but he couldn't stop them anymore than he could stop the feelings Marley evoked.

He'd lived through too many revolting things, seen the worst that one human could do to another. Images, he wished he could forget but knew he never would. It took a lot out of him, but he'd learn to handle the memories and live on his own terms, finding happiness and joy in simple things and seeing beauty again.

He knew for certain the greatest pleasure he would ever find was in the woman leaning against him. It was as if his soul called to her and hers answered. Zan wasn't sure when he'd turned so poetic but knew with every fiber of his body it was true.

He took the next curve and the view of the ocean opened up before them. The sun was beginning to touch the water. It wouldn't take long to set, not like in the mountains where the sunset lingered on.

He signaled and pulled off into a roadside viewpoint. Lowering his feet to the ground, he balanced the bike then placed his hands over Marley's, holding her tight to him as she leaned against him. In silence, they watched the sun dip and settle into the ocean. Its final rays spearing light tinged with orange, across the sky. When it disappeared completely, he restarted the motorcycle and headed for the small town nestled on the coast just a couple miles away.

The steakhouse sign caught his attention, and he pulled off again. "What do you think? I bet they have steak fries," he said over his shoulder.

"Sounds good to me," she answered with a light laugh that turned into a groan when she tried to stand.

"You okay?" Zan asked in alarm.

She stretched and groaned again. "I'm stiff." She reached for him, laying her hand on his bicep. "How's your shoulder?"

Its ache was closer to a throb, and as soon as they sat down to eat, he planned to take some more Ibuprofen, but he could handle it. What he needed was sleep, but first he had to have food. "It's okay. But I'm starving."

"That's always a good sign. I take it you're in the mood for a real big steak?"

"Yes, ma'am. Medium rare."

ଔଛ

Dinner passed quickly. Marley couldn't believe how

hungry she was, cleaning every bite off her plate. What surprised her more was the quaint little inn Zan stopped at instead of one of the big national chains.

She didn't comment when he slid his arm around her, walking her in like they were a loving couple. She wasn't even surprised when Zan asked for a suite, though she figured the man at the desk thought they were having an affair when Zan paid in cash. Still, nothing mattered when they walked into the cozy room with a view out toward the ocean.

"Oh, this is beautiful." She let her gaze drift over the room done in warm earth tones mixed with light blue, which during the day probably seemed to carry the beach and sky right inside.

Sheer white curtains billowed at the windows caught by the slight ocean breeze, framing the view of moonlight on the surf. Marley let her gaze drift over the room once more then stepped into the bathroom to take in the large tiled bath with two showerheads.

"Oh, yes," she exclaimed as a feeling of utter bliss filled her.

"Can I guess you want a shower?" Zan stood just behind her, looking over her shoulder.

"Want is not even close. And there's a toilet."

"Aren't you easy to please. I will even throw in a toothbrush."

"My hero." She smiled up at him. "Do you mind if I take the first shower?"

"Not at all. I'll just stretch out on the bed while you do. Then after, you can take the bed, and I'll shift over to the couch."

Marley figured she'd wait and fight him over that arrangement when she got out of the shower, because there was no way the couch would be comfortable for him. During her shower she decided it would be easiest to be already asleep in the hide-a-bed when he got out of the shower. As tired as she felt, it shouldn't be any problem and Zan wouldn't have the heart to shift her if she was asleep.

Marley washed her hair three times with the herbal shampoo provided by the inn, then basked a couple minutes longer under the warm water before she guiltily decided she'd better get out and give Zan a turn.

She paused in the motion of drying off, amazed at how comfortable it was having him out there. A week ago, it would have been way out of her comfort zone to be in a hotel room with a man.

Marley looked at herself in the mirror. She had changed so much in the last couple days, and Zan wasn't just any man. She felt a tug on her heart. Steadying herself, she pulled on the luxurious, white spa robe supplied by the inn. Picking up the brush, she started to work it through her hair as she stepped from the bathroom.

The sight of Zan stretched across the bed stopped her in her tracks. Even in sleep there was fierceness in his countenance but it didn't detract from his chiseled good-looks that caught her breath. Unable to stop herself, Marley settled on the edge of the bed.

Her fingers hover over his face a full minute before she got enough nerve to brush them over his cheek. The stubble on his chin was abrasive but intriguing at the same time. She stroked it, mesmerized by the feel.

Marley jerked back her hand realizing what she was doing. Her eyes went to his, expecting them to be watching her with either an accusing or amused expression. Fortunately, instead of finding him staring back at her, he remained asleep, his breathing coming deep and regular.

Marley smiled. The debate over the bed no longer a moot point when she tried to wake him so he could take his shower. Exhaustion had claimed his body in much needed rest. Marley smiled again as she removed his boots and socks before covering him up and going to bed herself.

03❦80

Sunlight filled the room, easing Marley from sleep. She shifted in bed and froze at the sight of Zan standing at the window, brooding at the bright, sunny morning, all remnants of the storms gone except for the one brewing inside him.

Marley pulled the robe on over the T-shirt she'd slept in before she stood. "Zan?" She moved around the end of the hide-a-bed to stand behind him.

He was dressed. His hair was wet from the shower. He looked like a stone centurion staring out at sea.

"Is something wrong?"

"No." The answered was clipped.

"Is your shoulder bothering you?"

He glanced down at it as if just noticing that it was to be of concern then looked back out the window. "No."

"Zan, what's wrong?"

She braved his stern demeanor to lay a hand on his shoulder. The muscles felt like iron – strong, unyielding. Marley found she couldn't stand to see him like that anymore than she could stand to see him in pain.

"Zan?" She let her hand slide down to the center of his back and raised her other hand next to it.

She could swear he stiffened more, but she didn't know how that could be possible. Leaning forward, she rested her cheek in the middle of his back. He started to move away, but she gripped the material, clamping down. "No, just stop it."

"What do you want from me?" he demanded sharply.

"I want to know what's bothering you," Marley answered just as crisply.

He shot a look over his shoulder, then turned back to the window. The answer came in a deep low rumble. "I fell asleep."

Marley felt even more confused. "So, it was night. We were supposed to sleep."

"You took off my boots."

Marley still knew she was missing something but couldn't figure out what. "I figured you'd be more comfortable."

"I didn't even notice." The words burst from him. "I'm usually a light sleeper in combat situations."

"I wouldn't quite call this combat."

He glared back over his shoulder at her. "I can go days without sleep."

Getting frustrated Marley moved around to stand in front of him. "You were shot, and you did go days without sleep."

He still refused to look down at her. "I wasn't alert enough to protect you."

As the words cut from him in sharp, pained syllables, Marley finally understood. Slowly, as if handling a wild animal, she eased her hand to his cheek. "I didn't need protection last night. I was safe. Because of what you did. And, I have no doubt, if danger had come, you would've awakened to protect me."

He might have been like a statue, but the stone was warm under her touch. When he slowly tilted his head down to look at her, the fire that she'd come to recognize was back in his eyes.

"You are too trusting."

"No," she answered truthfully.

But he continued his thought. "Beautiful, sweet, innocent, good. A world away from the life I've led." Pain slashed through the depth of his eyes.

She cradled his cheek in her palm. "Don't go there. You're a good man, Zan Masters."

He raised his hand up to cover hers. "You don't know the kind of man I am."

"Yes, I do." She held his gaze. "You're a man of honor, with a code embedded so deep it's in every breath you take."

"I want a relationship with you. But, when this is over, you're not going to want anything to do with all that's happened and the memories of it, which means me."

"You're wrong. You're the only man I've ever wanted a relationship with. And that is not going to change. You're my hero, not my nemesis."

"Is that why you want me, because I've become your personal hero?" He pulled away slightly.

"No. I don't want you because you saved me, because you've become 'my personal hero'. I want you," she paused. "I'm not even sure how to explain. I usually stutter horribly around dominant, powerful people. Good looking men make it worse. With you, I don't."

His lips quirked a little. "So you like me because you can talk to me?" One eyebrow arched up.

"Yes, but its more. I feel … whole with you. Does that make me sound pathetic? It's not, I'm not. I'm quite content in my life. I've just never fallen in love be–"

"Doc, you talk too much." He cut her off, his mouth covering hers. His fingers speared through her hair to cradle the back of her head.

Her arms slid up around his neck. Her world tilted and realigned with pleasure as the kiss continued on. Marley had no idea how much time passed when his mouth tore from hers. By the time she steadied herself, he stood several feet away. It took her still another minute to get his name out. "Zan?"

He shook his head. "No, Marley."

"I don't understand. What's wrong with kissing me?"

He glanced across the room to where it opened to the bedroom. He looked back at her. "I want you too much. But there are a lot of things you don't understand. I'm not very good at relationships."

He shifted his stance, as if standing at attention. His hands clasped behind his back. He drew in a deep breath.

"I've been married twice. My first wife was what you

could call a military junkie. Hung out at the places the guys hung out on their down times. We met, dated a couple months. I was young, head over heels, thought all was good. We got married then I got deployed for about six months, came back to find her four months pregnant. We got divorced, and she married the other guy."

"With my next wife," he went on without breaking. "I went to the other extreme. She was a secretary I met on a blind date. I figured I'd hurried things too fast before, so I dated her for two years. We got married, and things seemed okay. I got transferred overseas. I learned from my mistakes and took her with me. She handled it for about three months and wanted to come back. She made it two more months before she did. I finished the time there, but there was nothing for us when I got home. We divorced, and she remarried six months later to a nice guy who sold insurance."

He shrugged. "After that, I tried the happy bachelor life, but it isn't for me." He looked over her shoulder, out the window. "I guess you could say I'm not the girl in every port type. There is only one port in the storm for me." He shifted his gaze back to her. "I think I've finally found it."

Marley could hardly take in what he was saying. "You can't mean ... you can't be serious, about me." She didn't dare believe. "We just barely met."

"Yes. But that doesn't seem to change what is. In my other marriages, there was something missing. I should have seen it but didn't." His eyes smoldered with blue fire.

"I never wanted either of them like I want you, and I'm not talking sexually. Though, I'd be lying if I said I didn't find you desirable. Believe me, I do. But it's something more. It calls to me. Over the years, I've learned to listen to my instincts, and they're screaming at me that you're mine. Does that scare you?" His gaze bore down on her.

"Yes." The word slipped truthfully out her mouth,

followed slowly by another answer. "And no."

ભ૪

Zan felt heat flare in him, and he started to cross the floor. Sunlight came through the window, framing Marley, but the radiance from within her outshone it. She was his, though it wasn't time to make her so. There was so much they had to do first, but he vowed they'd have a future together.

"Just so you know. I'm going to kiss you again now, and then I'm going to release you because we have to keep our heads clear." He growled, clamping his hands on her shoulders.

She bit her lip then smiled at his declaration. "Just so you know. I haven't had a lot of experience kissing. I wasn't kidding when I said I've been kissed more in the last couple days than I have in my entire life."

A wicked pleasure flashed through him. "It's okay, Doc. This is something I know I can tutor you in." He pulled her up then shifted his hands to frame her face.

Her amber eyes caught and held, drawing him in.

Still concerned that he was hurrying her, he watched for fear and resistance as he lowered his head. None came. Marley rested her hands on his chest but not to push him away. Her arms slid deliciously slow around him. Her eyes darted from his, down to his lips, then back up to his eyes.

At the first touch of her lips, he felt warm silk. As it deepened, he tasted honey. Her eyes drifted closed, and she gave herself over to him to drink more fully.

He fought the need to ravish and sate his hunger. He slowed and sipped, teaching her lips to move with his. She thoroughly responded. Even after his kisses of the last two days, her inexperience was obvious, though how such a beautiful woman could have no experience was beyond him.

With each touch she seemed to come alive and gain confidence. He was losing his head to her. Reluctantly, he drew back before things could get out of hand. He pressed her to his chest, feeling her heart pound against him.

"Oh, sweetheart." He brushed his lips to her forehead. "If you keep learning like that, you'll have your doctorate in kissing in no time." Her face pressed into him and he felt the shake of her laughter.

"I told you, I always got the best schools and the best teachers. I think I was just waiting for the best instructor in this. The only other kisses I've had seemed dull and boring. I figured there must be something wrong with me. That I was too analytical." The words were hushed with self-doubt.

"You don't think my kisses are boring?" he pressed.

"Oh, no." She shook her head, rubbing her cheek against the wall of his chest. She tilted her face up to look at him. Her eyes blazed like molten honey. The corners of her lips tilted up.

"I find the subject of kissing you most titillating," she said brazenly. A blush snuck up to add color to her cheeks. "I think." She stumbled slightly over the word. "I'm going to need more in-depth learning."

"It's a good thing I plan to offer upper level courses then, but I'll warn you, the lab work is exacting. It may take a great amount of time and be exhausting."

"Is it worth it?" The words, this time, were whispered with excitement.

"Oh yes," he growled out. "I guarantee it." He pulled her up to meet his lips again, only to rip them back away, tucking her under his chin. "It's okay, sweetheart. We need to slow down. I didn't expect it to be so explosive." He felt her jerk at his choice of words.

She pulled back. "Zan, being around me is dangerous."

"I think I just figured that out." He grinned trying to make light of it.

"No, I'm serious."

"I know, but the only thing that it changes is, that for

now, unfortunately, school's out. Why don't you get dressed? I'll order us some breakfast, then we'll see if we can't get a hold of the General."

To her credit, Marley nodded and stepped from his arms. At the bathroom door, she stopped and looked back at him. There was worry but such unmistakable love in her eyes, his heart soared.

As the door closed behind her, it hit him again that after all the ugliness he'd experienced in his life, how someone so good could want him. He wished he could shelter her from the evil but couldn't. Still, there was one thing good in all this. Marley was his.

CʒѢ

Marley sagged back against the bathroom door not sure what was happening to her. Everything was topsy-turvy. She was in love and kissing a man who was a virtual stranger to her. It didn't seem to matter that people were trying to kill her because she had information that could destroy her company and ruin many people's lives. All she could think of, for the moment, was she loved Zan and he loved her.

No one had ever loved her before. Oh, her parents did and her grandparents. She knew that, but it seemed she spent so much time off and away from them growing up that the connection was different.

She always wondered if her brain made her different – made it that she could never have romantic love. That maybe she was just too logical for love. No. She looked at herself in the mirror. She'd always believed in love, just had given up on it happening to her.

CʒѢ

Breakfast was a delight which they shared at the table in their room with the warm ocean air wafting in through the windows. It would have been perfect but Zan was stiff again. Marley paused, her last bite of crepes filled with strawberries and whipped cream an inch from her mouth, and set her fork down.

"Zan?"

This time he didn't try to ignore the question in his name. "I'm sorry."

"What is it?"

He reached out, taking her hand, rubbing his thumb over her knuckles. "Probably nothing, but the more I think about it, the more I can't let it go."

"What?"

"While you were changing, I tried to call General Gallup again. I was told that he wasn't there, that he'd gone to the base not far from here. It's where we're headed."

"Then that's good."

"No. I don't think so. I was taking us there because it's the closest Army facility. The more I think about it, it's too convenient for the exact person you want to see will be there. It doesn't make sense. Why would he be there?"

"What do you mean? Why wouldn't he?" She tilted her head to the side, clearly confused.

"It's an Army base. He's Air Force. Even if he was in a joint meeting, I can't see it being there."

Marley got what he was saying. "You think someone told you wrong to mislead you?" Marley could see his mind reworking over the question.

He nodded slowly. "I do. It's reasonable that I would find an Army base more comfortable, so I would likely head there," he continued as his mind connected unseen dots in a pattern. "But the area around it is more deserted or maybe I should say out of the way. It would be easier to track us and set up an ambush." He stood abruptly. "We need to go."

"Zan?"

"I think my call may have been traced."

"Can they trace a disposable?"

"They can trace any phone. I was just hoping to buy us some time not having one in my name since they would have had that info by investigating who owned my house."

Marley was already up, following his lead, grabbing her stuff to throw into his backpack.

"Where we going?" she asked over her shoulder.

"South, then we'll have a couple of options to make a run for. Hopefully, we can throw whoever's after us off. We need to get you to a base and talk to the commander there and get you some more protection as soon as possible."

Marley stepped into the bathroom to retrieve her brush and came out with the first aid kit. "I should check your shoulder first."

"I already took care of it when I showered."

"I hope you didn't get it wet."

"Don't worry, Marley, I know what to do and I was careful." He caught her by the arm, turning her to face him. "I plan on a long life teaching you all sorts of new things."

"That's right." She forced out a brave smile. "And don't you forget any. And, I want a dance."

"It is one of the first activities on my agenda." He twirled her into him, kissed her then spun her back out.

"That doesn't count," she countered, grabbing up the leather jacket.

"It was just a promise. Ready?"

"Yes." She snatched up the last bite of crepe from her plate and popped it in her mouth on her way out the door, with one last look at the charming room. "It was so nice," she commented forlornly as she met his stride.

"We can come back sometime if you'd like." Zan caught her elbow, halting her. He glanced down the hall before turning the corner. Tension radiated off him. He was back on full alert.

Marley felt her senses heighten.

Since Zan had paid the night before, it only took him a minute to pay for their room service and hand in the key. They pulled on their helmets before exiting a side door.

Keeping close to the building, they hurried to where they'd left the motorcycle tucked in at the end between a truck and the bushes. There was no hesitation in Marley now as she climbed on behind him and wrapped her arms around his waist.

They headed out along the coast highway. Marley usually admired how beautiful it was along this section of the coast but today it had an ominous taint to it. Because of the ocean to the west and the rugged mountain range on the east which only allowed limited access with a handful of roads, they were relatively trapped.

She knew Zan worried about it because it meant whoever was after her only had to keep watch on a couple roads. Now she understood why Zan was so cautious at setting up a disguise for them on the motorcycle. She also knew it wouldn't take long for those after them to recognize them. They had bought one night of peace, but from here on out, they were in for a difficult race, as if the last couple days had been easy.

She glanced at the ocean, seeing the water roll in, hit the rocks, and spray up. Around the next point, sand stretched out in a secluded, inviting beach, protected by a ridge of rocks and brush. Marley wished they could pull over and hide out there until the danger passed, but she wondered when that would be. How long would they hunt for her and Zan?

Sadly she knew they would never let up in the search for her, and there wasn't time to wait, they had to get the information out. The longer they waited the more lives could be risked on experimentation of the drug. Panic began to rise within her. Marley wanted to press her face into Zan's back, but the helmet was in the way. Still, she took comfort with him there in front of her.

Chapter Ten

Zan felt the tension ebb and flow from Marley's body and wished he could pull over, take her in his arms, and reassure her all was going to be all right. The only thing was, it wasn't something he could be certain of. His self-arrogance declared he wouldn't let anything happen to her, he couldn't. She was everything he'd been looking for and hadn't even known he was searching. Still, he knew what they were facing and knew it would take all his skills to keep them alive.

Zan eased up on the gas, giving them a second to take in the peace and beauty of the morning and the fresh air with a tang of salt off the ocean. Marley hugged him tight. Some of the tension seemed to ease in her body.

He removed his left hand from the handlebars long enough to lay it over hers and give it a squeeze. She returned the action with a light pressure on his ribs. He savored the moment before placing his hand back on the handlebars.

Six more miles ahead they came around a bend and Zan caught a glimpse of a black SUV with dark tinted windows parked in a roadside turnout. A spike of concern surged in him but faded when he didn't see the SUV pull out in the rearview mirror. Still, he had to fight the urge to put on more speed.

The road straightened out before them. Zan shifted his attention again to the mirror, glancing back to the road, then back to the mirror. He looked up again just in time to see another identical black SUV, come around the curve a half mile in front of them. A quick glance in the mirror revealed the first vehicle as it came around the corner behind them, gaining fast.

"Hold on," he yelled over his shoulder, not sure if Marley caught the words before the wind whipped them away. But, when he leaned forward over the handlebars, she followed the action, tightening her hold.

He eased up slightly on the gas, and the SUV behind them began to gain as the one ahead grew closer. There was only one other vehicle in sight. A little red Volkswagen Beetle with it's top down and three young women in it, just in front of the SUV coming toward them.

Zan slowed as he approached the Beetle. When he was only about thirty feet from it, he goosed the gas and swerved in front of the little red car. He caught the screams of the girls as he and Marley whipped by on the edge of the road. Then they were beside the SUV.

The windows were down, illuminating the interior. Zan made out the images of two men as they shot past. He caught the outline of a gun in the passenger's hand, but the driver swerved to avoid hitting the red car that had slammed on its brakes, giving him no chance to fire.

Pulling back on the road, they barely missed the back end of the SUV as it fishtailed slightly. Clear, Zan put on more speed, drifting back to the center of the road. The SUV from behind sped past the other two vehicles. Zan squeezed the gas down all the way.

They pulled away for a brief second then the black monster with its huge engine began to close the gap. They came to a curve, and Zan eased a little on the gas, still, he took it faster than he preferred with Marley on back. Fortunately, she had molded herself along his back, following his movement as if in an intricate dance. The big vehicle had to slow down more on the curve, but the time they gained was short lived as the space once again narrowed.

They'd made it around another curve when Zan caught the black dot of the other SUV rejoining the chase, then his attention locked on the one moving up on him. The bike was going full out, but it was obvious there was no way they were going to outrun them on the straight away.

Zan looked for other options. A small town sat as a beacon just ahead, but there was no way they were going to make it there before they were overtaken. He barely noticed the sign indicating a beach turn out just ahead. The SUV was nearly beside them when Zan let up on the gas and carefully squeezed down on the brake while turning into the parking lot.

Behind him, Marley locked tight to his body to keep from being swung off as the bike skidded slightly, but she stayed with him. The SUV shot past the turnoff as Zan accelerated into the parking lot. Brakes squealed on the road, and a hand with a gun extended out the window.

Zan ignored the shot that ricocheted off the blacktop in front of the bike. Another sounded behind them. Keeping the gas steady, he shot past the sign declaring no motorized vehicles on the beach, easing only slightly to veer through the access dip in the curb.

Sand rooster-tailed up behind, but Zan kept the power steady, taking them out over the beach, angling to the water's edge where the sand was better packed. A glance to the side revealed the other vehicle had joined the first. One shot ahead while the other paralleled them. Fortunately, the distance was enough and there were too many shrubs for them to get a shot off. Zan had no delusion to the fact that he was marked for death so they could get a hold of Marley, and they needed her alive only long enough to get the information she had.

The temptation for more speed ate at him, but he knew they were better off on the sand where they were. They just needed to reach town and find some place to hide before the other SUV could cut them off. Ahead the town reached out welcoming. People started to dot the sand. Several yelled for them to get off the beach as they passed, but unfortunately, none were police, though Zan wasn't sure if they'd be much help from the people after Marley.

Zan reached the beach parking lot on the edge of town just as the familiar black SUV sped into it. Zan swung wide back down by the water just as a wave came in, sending up a light spray. He slowed to angle around a rock outcropping which would have cut them off if it was high tide, but now gave them shelter from the view of the men in the parking lot.

Another three hundred yards along the beach, Zan spied an opening between two beach houses. He changed direction, driving up over a small patio and down a driveway onto the street. He gave the bike a little more gas, weaving through the streets. Marley tapped his arm and pointed to a house with a for sale sign in front. He whipped into the driveway, stopping the bike behind a huge Oleander bush in the corner of the yard.

He balanced the motorcycle between his feet and cut the motor. Not making any movement to dismount, he waited for several minutes before raising his windscreen and looking back over his shoulder.

"Are you all right?"

Marley followed his motion in raising her shield. "Yes." She swung her leg over the back and stood none too steady. "They found us." Fear rang in her words.

"Unfortunately, we seemed to hit a day of light traffic."

"What do we do now?"

"We'll wait here for a while then try to make our way around them to the road."

"You don't think that will work?" she asked, as if reading his thoughts.

"They have us cut off this way, and they know it. They just have to wait on the road on the other side of town and they'll see us." He was quiet a minute before he spoke again. "Either they have both directions covered, which is likely, or they figured I'd make a run south because there is more traffic and roads down there to get lost in. I also would have had more base options to make a run to, plus a number more the farther south."

"So again, what do we do?"

He took a second to pull off his helmet and get off the bike to stand in front of her. He waited as she took off her helmet and set it down. "We'll make an attempt to get past them, and if we can't, we'll head the other way."

"You think they'll be waiting."

"Yes."

"I'm so sorry, Zan." A tear slipped from the corner of her eye.

He wrapped his arms around her and pulled her to him. "It's all right. We'll make it." When she didn't say anything, he eased back, cupping her cheek in his palm, lifting her face to meet his kiss. He let it continue until he drew out a shiver that had nothing to do with fear and danger. He broke the kiss and leaned his head down to rest on hers. "We'll make it," he repeated.

"This still seems so unreal, people dying, you getting shot, and those men after us. I don't know what to do." She wrapped her arms around him, snuggling in.

He kissed her temple, bringing her tighter. Funny, to him it felt natural. He'd spent most of his life with people trying to kill him, though the reward was much more personal to him now. "Just have faith in me."

"That's the only thing I do have." She raised her head meeting his gaze, love and trust shown in her eyes for him to see. "Why couldn't we have met in some nice normal way, like running our carts into each other at the grocery store?"

"Maybe, because we weren't looking, so fate had to hit us over the head." He gave her a lop-sided grin.

"You believe in fate?"

"I believe certain things are meant to be. And I believe I was meant to find you."

"I can't believe after all I've brought upon you, you can mean that." Her eyes searched his face for reassurance.

He smiled. "I mean it. And I plan on taking a lot of reward from you for years to come."

"Oh, you do."

"Yes." He kissed her, backing up the word with a hint of what he was meaning.

"Excuse me." There was a clearing of the throat along with the words.

Marley's cheeks turned pink in embarrassment. All Zan felt was annoyance at the interruption, though he had to admit it was for the better.

"I don't think anyone's around to show you the house today." An older woman with a shaggy little dog on a leash looked them up and down. Her nose wrinkled disapprovingly.

Zan almost laughed at the woman, thinking the dog, with a bright pink bow on the top of its head, wouldn't be much of a deterrent if they were up to no good. Though, he had to give it to the woman for being brave enough to approach them. He figured most people would've called the police if they did anything. Then again, she might have called before approaching them.

"Yes, we figured that out. My wife and I saw the sign and just had to stop and check it out. We're looking for something in this area." He lied smoothly, though it took considerable effort to keep a straight face at the woman's obvious horror at the thought. "We have the number," he pulled his cell phone out of his pocket and held it up, "so we can call on it later."

The woman eyed the phone then them. "Yes, well

good-bye. Come on, Precious." She pulled the dog around and marched off.

Zan watched the woman disappear on the other side of the bushes. A small giggle from behind had him turning. Marley had a hand over her mouth. Her eyes twinkled with mirth above her fingers.

He arched an eyebrow at her. "I don't think she's excited to have us as neighbors."

Laughter escaped Marley.

Zan felt like going after the woman and thanking her for lightening Marley's mood but figured they'd better get out of there just in case she had called the police. "Come on." He picked up her helmet, putting it over her head then snuck in through the shield opening to give her one last swift kiss before setting his own helmet on his head.

They rode out of the subdivision, each keeping an eye out for the SUVs. They made their way along side streets to the east side of the town, then worked their way to where the last street came out to join up to the highway. Luckily, the road sat on a slight rise, giving them a view of the highway and ocean. Zan stopped the motorcycle and studied the stretch of highway extending along the beach. A half mile down, he caught the glint of sunlight off of chrome.

"Do you think we can make it past them on the beach like we did getting here?" Marley asked.

"No, they have a direct view of the beach and the road. They'd be right on us, and they have a lot more horsepower than the bike does." He thought for a minute more and pulled the cell phone out of his pocket, turning it back on. "I want to try calling the General again."

"I thought you were afraid of it being traced?"

"They already know we're here, and we'll move as soon as I hang up. I just want to see if I can get through and if we get any reaction from our friends down there."

He dialed a number then asked for a transfer. After a

second he said, "This is Lieutenant Colonel Zan Masters. I'd like to speak to General Gallup." When he was put on hold, Zan started to count. He was just about to hang up when another voice came over the line.

"Masters. This is Major Snyder. I'm an aide to General Gallup. The General is tied up in meetings. How can I help you?"

The hair on Zan's nape stood up. He watched two seconds tick down on his watch. "It is top priority that I speak directly with General Gallup."

"That is impossible right now. If you'd like to leave a message."

Zan knew the man was stalling. "I'll call back." He cut the connection, turned off the phone and removed the battery.

"Zan?"

"No go. Come on. Let's head back down by the beach."

"You gave them your name?"

"I figure from here on out there isn't any point not to. They already have that information."

✂✄

"Maybe you should just take me to the police station." Marley hated the idea because she knew she'd be separated from Zan, but the thought of him in danger hurt her more.

He was already shaking his head before she finished the sentence. "I don't think that's a good idea. Those after you have connections. You could end up disappearing from the police station without anyone being the wiser. We stick with the plan and get you to a base."

He started the bike. Again, they wove their way through the streets, careful to stay within the speed limit and not do anything that would attract attention. There was no sign of the other SUV, but Zan didn't doubt they were out there looking.

When they got to the congested area where shops lined

the beach, Zan pulled around behind a weathered building that rented surfboards, skates and water crafts. This time, he parked along a row of bougainvillea that divided the shop from the one next door.

"What are we going to do?" Marley asked, which was feeling like an all too familiar question.

"Hang out here for a little while. Let our searchers worry about if they missed us and get tired and hungry." He reached for the backpack, easing it off her shoulders.

Marley took off her leather jacket and folded it into her helmet. Zan studied the light weight sweater approvingly. The upper part was loose, draping over her shoulders in an appealing way. The bottom hugged her waist accentuating her shape. It worked for Marley and the beach. They just needed a couple added items.

Zan took her hand, leading her out into the crowd. He stopped at a street vendor and negotiated for a pair of sunglasses for each of them. At the next vendor, he bought her a white cloth hat with a wide, floppy brim and for himself, a cap with a popular sports logo on it. They then joined a group sitting on the grass under a palm tree, listening to a trio of street musicians.

Marley felt herself relax though she knew Zan stayed alert, his eyes constantly drifting over the people and watching the parking areas. His arm wrapped around her back, his hand on her waist, keeping her snug against him. It was a possessive touch that Marley found comforting, though she didn't think he was really aware of doing it. The music set ended, he shifted and clapped automatically with the crowd but his attention was focused in the distance.

He leaned closer to speak in her ear. "It's about lunch time. How do you feel about fish and chips?"

She laughed. "You know I don't have to have fries for every meal."

"Okay, something green for you and fish and chips for me. You stay here in the crowd where you blend in but you're not out of my sight. I'm just going over there." He pointed to a couple of eating places. "If anyone comes near, you scream or make a scene. I'll be watching."

"Okay."

He gave her a kiss, as seemed to be natural for him now, and stood. Marley felt a wave of unease as he walked away. She tried to concentrate on the music but her attention remained with Zan.

He stopped for a minute at an information board before making his way through the outdoor seating area, where he stopped to talk to a young man who seemed to be playing a game on a cell phone. After a minute, Zan took out his wallet and removed a bill, handing it to the youth, who handed over his cell phone.

Marley watched Zan put in a number, wait a minute then start talking. As the conversation went on, Marley wondered who he was talking to. Hope surged that maybe he was finally able to get a hold of the General.

As soon as the thought came to her, she discounted it. Something told her Zan wouldn't try to contact him again until he had her safely tucked away on a military base somewhere where he thought she was safe. She shivered at the thought of being confined, and used the knowledge that Zan would be with her to ease the fear.

The next song ended. She applauded with the rest of the people. Finally, Zan handed the phone back to the youth and went into the restaurant. He came out a few minutes later with two metal pans and two large drinks. Though he appeared casual in his movements, his stride still ate up the distance until he was back to her.

"What's that?" she greeted him, taking the drinks.

"That is a pink-lemonade for you. Your preference if I remember right. And, that is a sweet-pork salad." He handed her an aluminum tin. "For me, there's a burrito Grande." He lowered himself back down by her.

"The call?"

"I paid the kid ten bucks to use his phone to call my old commander. I was actually able to get through to him. He's back in the states."

She reached out to catch his hand. "Zan?"

"I filled him in on what's happening. He's going to take it to his superior and see what he can get rolling."

"Then at least it's out." Marley felt a weight ease on her.

Zan caught her hand, rubbing his thumb over her knuckles. "Yes, but they still need you and the proof. Otherwise there can be an argument that it was all fabricated by a disgruntled employee."

"Still, if–"

"Don't even go there." He cut her off, squeezing her hand lightly.

"Okay, so what do we do? Wait here for help?"

"No, it's hard to say how long it could take. We can't risk being out here that long. So first, we're going to eat our lunch and relax a little longer. Then, we're going to go recheck the road leading out of town and a mountain road I found on the map." He opened the map he'd gotten from the information board and pointed to a line. "If it's blocked, as I'm guessing it is, we'll head back the other way and make a run north."

"North?"

"There's an army base. Mainly, they teach linguistics to all branches. I thought of it once, but it made more sense to go south because there are more options. Eat." He nodded to her food.

Marley forked up a mouth full of the salad. "Oh, this is good."

"Better than MREs?" Zan teased.

"I'm afraid so. It's hard to believe that was just two days ago. How's yours?"

"Good. You want a try?" He held out his fork loaded with meat, beans and a piece of tortilla shell.

Marley only paused a second before she leaned closer and opened her mouth for him to place it in. His eyes seemed to grow more intense as he watched her.

"What do you think?" A husky tone filled his voice, making the words seem to rumble out.

"So good."

Marley felt the heat flare between them and, for a minute, forgot all about her salad and everything else but Zan. The applause from the crowd around them brought her back to the present.

"I-I," she stumbled getting the words out and realized she hadn't stuttered around Zan all day. Or, if she had, she hadn't realized it. She took a deep breath and let it out slowly with the words gliding along with the breath. "We'd better eat." She turned her attention back to the food and music, listening for a few minutes before she glanced over at him. "Tell me about your brother?" she asked just wanting to hear his voice. "Are you a lot alike?"

"Oh yeah." Zan leaned close to her, sheltering her with his body. "We were always very close. Not at all competitive with each other. If we ever had the tendency our mom nipped it in the bud when we were young. We were best friends. If one of us got into trouble, the other was right there in it too."

"Did you get into trouble often?" She tried to picture him as a boy. He'd have been busy, played hard, and been a good friend and brother.

"Not really, but we were boys." His lips twitched at some memory.

Marley was tempted to ask what it was but changed her mind. "So you both joined the Army?"

"Yes, right out of school."

"And you both ended up in Special Forces."

"Yes." He looked a little more serious. "We'd done our own thing for a while. I'd just finished my first degree and Zac's marriage just ended in a divorce about that time. My second one was long over. Neither of us had real good luck with marriage, so you know what you're getting into. But, I guess that's a discussion for another time."

Marley felt a catch in her heart, wondering what he meant. She cleared her throat. "So neither of you had children?"

"No, fortunately. Anyway, Zac and I got together and were talking about things, careers, life, and decided maybe we were meant to be alone. To make it short, we decided since we were single to do the ranger training. We had all the qualifications. We both passed the test. Next six months we went through more training and we both made it through ranger school."

"Something tells me it's not as easy as you just made it sound."

He gave her a wry smile. "It's not."

She tilted her head to the side studying him. "I saw a documentary once on Navy seal training."

He nodded, "It's similar. We're medically trained first responders, jump out of perfectly good airplanes at any height, taught man-to-man, light artillery, explosives, etc."

"Well rounded." She looked at him.

"They don't lie. They promise you will be put in harm's way. Ranger's lead the way."

"So you're used to walking into danger." She swallowed and turned her attention back to the musicians.

His hand settles over hers and squeezed her fingers. He waited until she looked at him. "I'm going to do everything I can to keep you safe, Marley."

"I know. It's just … I don't want you in danger because of me."

"It is my choice and I want to be here with you."

Marley felt tears well up within her and turned her attention back to her food, using it as a distraction while she got herself under control.

They finished their meal in silence. Zan stood and

stepped through the crowd to drop some money in the open guitar case then returned to her, holding out his hand. Again, Marley felt a tingle of awareness but no fear as his powerful, callused hand closed around hers. With a light tug, he pulled her up, sliding his arm around her as he turned her toward where they'd left the motorcycle.

They'd only covered about half the distance when Marley saw a black vehicle turn on to the boulevard.

"Zan!"

"I see it. Just keep walking." He leaned his body over hers slightly in a protective movement as he eased them through the crowd toward the closest shop.

"Do you think they saw us?"

"No. In the mood for some dessert?" he asked as they stepped inside.

Marley laughed as tension released from her body. "You think I have a weakness for French fries, it's nothing compared to how I feel about chocolate."

"Why, Doc."

"I'll have you know chocolate is a very important food group."

This time Zan laughed. It sounded rusty as if he didn't do it often. Still, amidst all that was happening, it made everything a bit better.

"By all means, don't let it be said I stood between a woman and her chocolate."

Marley stepped past him to the case, aware that most of his attention was focused outside. No matter what he said, he wasn't going to let his guard down. When she made her decision, Zan ordered two, not bothering to look at the case.

She accepted the small bag while he received the change. They stopped and stood just inside the front window.

"You know, I could have ordered chocolate covered ants," Marley said, feeling a bit mischievous among all the stress she was experiencing.

That got his attention, and he looked down at her. The corner of his lip curved up. "Somehow, I can't quite see that."

She smiled as the warmth in his gaze broke some of the tension. "You're right, just nuts."

They savored the chocolates, drawing the time out until they figured their presence was starting to look suspicious. At the corner of the building, they paused. Zan caught the attention of a boy about fifteen on a skateboard.

"Hey, can you do me a favor?"

The boy looked from Zan to Marley. She smiled and he relaxed a little. "Depends."

"Can you look around the edge of the building to the parking lot and road and see if there's a big, new, shiny black SUV with tinted windows out there?"

The boy looked at Zan again then at her and back to Zan. "You famous?"

"She is. I'm just her bodyguard. The guys in the SUV are hounding her."

The boy looked at her again as if trying to recognize who she was.

Marley had to fight to keep from laughing.

After a second the kid shrugged. "Sure." He stepped around the corner, studied the area then turned back. "Don't see any SUV."

"Thanks." Zan wrapped an arm around Marley's back, easing her out in the crowd. She held back, turning back to the boy. "Thank you." She gave him another smile, and he grinned back.

"Sure, no problem."

They fell into step with the crowd, letting it carry them toward the rental shop.

"So I'm famous." Marley reached for some lightness in the situation, as tension once again hummed in the air.

"Hey, it's the truth. Though, I guess I could have said

infamous."

Marley made a small snort. "I don't think of you as my bodyguard."

"But at the moment, that is what I am."

"Zan–" her protest was cut off with him pulling her forward.

"Come on."

They broke into a run fifteen feet from the rental building, dodging through people and around the corner to the motorcycle. Everything was as they had left it. A minute later, they were on the go.

After a quick stop at a gas station, they cut through town until they made it to the overlook they'd stopped at earlier where the streets petered out. The SUV was easily seen waiting just past the edge of town like a great lurking shadow.

Zan didn't say anything, just turned the bike and headed for the mountain road that would have been an alternative route. He slowed, cautious as they approached the mouth of the canyon. Zan swung off as he caught sight of a familiar looking vehicle on the side of the road up ahead.

"How m-many of those things do they have?" Marley said, loud enough for him to hear.

"They're pulling out all the stops for you, Doc."

"It's like they want us to know they're there."

"I think they do," he said simply, turning the bike around, cutting through side streets, heading north.

There was no sight of any telltale black vehicles as they turned out onto the highway. With each mile that passed, apprehension rose within Marley to meet the tautness in Zan. When they passed another small town, Marley tried to convince herself that they would actually make it. The thought shattered coming over the next rise and Marley once again spotted the now overly familiar black object beside the road.

Zan let up on the gas, easing over to the side of the road. As Marley watched, the SUV pulled forward a little, edging its nose onto the road. She knew Zan was debating if he could make it around it. Zan revved the engine, but before he let up on the clutch, the front passenger window rolled down. The distance was too far to make out the man in the seat, but she recognized the object in his hand.

Chapter Eleven

As the man brought the gun to level, Zan released the clutch, turning the bike in the same instant. The back tire skidded. Marley locked down on her hold. The motorcycle righted. They sped back the other way.

Marley remember seeing the road that would take them through the mountains a half mile back. She knew it would take them almost directly to the military base. She also knew why Zan hadn't taken it.

Now more than ever his theory of being herded that way was confirmed. She caught sight of the intersection as they went passed, not at all surprised when Zan didn't turn. What he had planned she didn't know, she just trusted him.

Marley wanted to see if they were being followed but, at the speed they were going, didn't dare look back, afraid of throwing Zan's balance off. It really didn't matter. She could feel them there, like little ants crawling up her skin.

One mile turned into four. Zan didn't let up on the gas. He pushed the motorcycle wide open. They came around a bend to where the road straightened out. On the east side of the road a campground offered a relaxing spot on the seaside, but all thoughts of peace were shattered for Marley at the sight of the menacing SUV directly in front of them.

Instead of slowing like Marley figured, Zan shifted to put on a little more speed. The engine screamed as the motorcycle leapt forward. The space between them and the SUV seemed to evaporate. The shiny metal grill morphed into a monstrous smile bearing down on them.

Marley caught her breath. The feeling of panic ate at her. She fought for calm, assuring herself that any second Zan would let up on the gas and swing them around. But he kept the speed on, leaning forward over the handlebars. Determination tensed in his body.

Marley tightened her hold, making herself ready for what Zan did next. She figured now she knew what it felt like to be in a joust, only she knew who would win if they impacted. With less than fifteen feet separating them, Zan suddenly let up on the gas, braked and swung the motorcycle directly in front of the SUV.

Marley screamed and clung to Zan. The image of the big vehicle charging down on them burned in Marley's mind so terrifyingly it took her a second to realize the SUV had passed, missing their back tire by no more than a foot to spare.

The squeal of brakes whined behind them as they sped up the small mountain road. Marley pressed into Zan's back. She should've been terrified as the road snaked around the side of the mountain. Though their pace was slower, trees and bushes seemed to fly by. Her heart pounded in her chest. She felt shaky and exhilarated all at once. Her mind diagnosed it as adrenaline rush, but it did little to ease the feeling.

They picked up speed on a longer, straighter stretch then slowed for an approaching curve. Marley took the opportunity to catch a glance over her shoulder. The road behind them was empty.

She wanted to believe they weren't being followed but knew better. It then dawned on her that they had the advantage now on the motorcycle. The big SUVs had them on power but were less maneuverable on the tight turns. The question was, would there be another of the black beasts with a loaded gun pointed at them waiting up ahead.

Time clicked off in her mind. Marley figured it had

been at least twenty minutes since they turned off the road, and there was still no sight of any other vehicles. She looked over at the scenery and wished they could just pull over and maybe take a hike, get lost in the trees where no one could find them.

The woods with Zan beside her held great appeal, which was probably silly after their frenzied flight though the woods and Zan getting shot just days earlier. But, to be away from everyone, especially away from danger, and have just the peace and beauty around them sounded so good.

Marley looked up at the clear blue sky and caught a glimpse of a large bird she decided was a hawk, since it looked like it had a neck and turkey vultures didn't. It soared out over the gully, catching an air current to hang effortlessly in the sky. She was so wrapped up in it, she almost missed the other object which swooped through the sky.

The helicopter banked over the ridge and swung toward them. Marley wanted to discount it but couldn't. Tightening one arm around Zan's waist, Marley released her hold with the other to tap Zan's arm and then point to the sky.

Zan let up the speed then followed her motion until he saw the copter closing in on them.

Marley wasn't sure if she heard him yell, "hold on," or if it was just her mind supplying it, but she barely got her arm back around him when the bike shot forward. Again, Zan leaned over the handlebars. Marley tried to follow his motions as the ground whipped by at dizzying speed. The helicopter roared as it skimmed passed just a couple feet over their heads then climbed straight up to miss a stand of trees that edged both sides of the road.

They followed the road as it curved around for about two hundred yards. When they came out of the trees, the helicopter was there waiting, hovering just a few feet off the ground. Zan continued on at full speed, swinging the motorcycle to the side, cutting just behind the skids of the helicopter.

Marley screamed and ducked as they cleared the tail section by only a foot. The blade at the end whipped the air only six feet away.

They didn't make it far before the helicopter buzzed over them again to hover just above the road. Marley could make out two men in front but their helmets and glasses made it impossible to recognize them, even if they were familiar. This time as they raced toward the helicopter, it dropped lower to the ground. Marley flinched afraid there was no way they could make it around it. Then, to make it worse, the side panel slid open revealing a third man with a gun.

For about another thirty feet, Zan kept them headed directly for the helicopter as if to repeat the maneuver he'd done previously. With just twenty feet to the copter, he turned the bike off the road. He eased up on the gas as they went up the small embankment that edged the road, but their momentum was enough that they still went airborne for several feet.

Marley closed her eyes as she felt herself lift off the seat of the bike then smack down as they landed. She felt the jolt through every fiber of her body. Against her will, her eyes sprung open, expecting to see them crash, but somehow Zan kept them upright.

The motorcycle bounced again over another rise. Marley, slightly unseated from the last landing, felt her foot slide off the foot-peg and fought to right herself without pulling Zan off with her. The bike slowed, as if Zan was going to stop, but as soon as her foot found its way back to the peg and she shifted into her seat, they picked up speed again.

Trees whipped by. Branches clawed at them, making Marley grateful for the leather jacket and helmet. Zan cut speed and twisted the handlebars hard to the right to avoid a downed log. Slower, they wove their way through a gully. Water sprayed up, soaking Marley's pant legs as they crossed through a stream.

Coming upon a large, steep bank, they climbed it slower so that the wheels remained on the ground. They were up it before Marley had too much of a chance to be afraid of falling off.

A small game trail led up the hill. Zan maneuvered them onto it, gave the motorcycle a little more gas and started to climb. Over the whine of the engine, Marley could still hear the beat of the helicopter.

Zan swung them around a rock ledge surrounded by tall trees. He braked, and they skidded to a stop. His feet dropped to the ground. He cut the motor, tensed and waited. For a moment, silence filled the woods then the thump, thump of the rotors sounded above the trees. Wind whipped the branches not far away.

"Zan," Marley cried out for him, fear flooding her.

"It's okay." His voice came back to her as steady as a brick wall. "They know we're here but can't see us. Catch your breath, and we'll see if they move on."

The way his hands remained poised on the handlebars said he really didn't believe it likely. Marley wished he would take them off and wrap his arms around her but had to be satisfied just holding him. Twice more the helicopter passed close overhead, but neither time were they able to see the craft before it drifted away.

When Zan released the handlebars to reach into his inside pocket, she leaned forward to get a look at what he had, catching a glimpse of a cell phone.

"What are you doing?"

"Playing a long shot."

"Can you get reception?"

"Not here." Instead of putting the phone back in his pocket, he lifted his pant leg and worked it down into his boot.

"What do we do now?" She finally ventured the question.

"Wait. There's no way we can outrun a helicopter. We have to keep them up there where they can't touch us. The problem is ground backup will be on its way, so we can't stay here too long." The words were hardly out of his mouth when the sound of the helicopter drew closer again.

"Hang on, time to go." Zan revved the motorcycle. It roared to life, and they were climbing again, angling across the side hill where the trees started to thin out.

A small dirt road cut across the trail. Zan dropped down on it, picking up speed. The helicopter was nowhere in sight. With all the switches, Marley had no idea what direction they were going but she was sure Zan knew.

They came to a fork in the road. Zan swung to the left without any hesitation. Marley was concentrating on watching the sky, the motorcycle jerked to the side almost unseating her, only locking her arms down around Zan's waist kept her from flying off. Her attention darted back to the road, and a cry of fear escaped her.

It wasn't a black SUV that sat angled across the road in front of them but the white vehicle that blocked the road was familiar as was the red and yellow logo of the lab in which she worked for emblazoned on the side. Zan let up on the speed, changing their direction, but instead of turning them in a complete circle, he headed them off the road again into the trees. The tires kicked up dirt as the bike climbed the small embankment.

Marley screamed as she heard the crack of a gunshot. The motorcycle jerked to the side. The next thing Marley knew she was ripped from the bike, airborne, still locked on Zan. Their landing was cushioned by a bush, but the impact felt like it jarred every bone in her body. Her ears rang. Shadows danced in front of her eyes. She was tempted to slide into the darkness and escape then she became aware of Zan calling her name.

The panic which filled his voice stabbed at her. She reached to soothe it. Forcing her eyes open, they were trapped in the glacial blue of his eyes that were anything but cold.

"Are you all right?" The words rushed from him, and it took her a second to decipher them. "Marley?" Her name came out demanding an answer.

"Yes." The word was as shaky as she felt. Marley started to sit up only to have Zan push her back down.

"No, stay still until I know you're all right." His attention shifted to his hands which ran up and down one leg and then the other before moving to repeat the process with her arms.

"Zan." She tried to pull up. "I'm all right. I was just a little stunned."

He ignored her, catching her helmet between his hands, looking into her eyes. "How's your vision? Are you seeing double?"

"No, I'm fine, but what about you? Your shoulder?" Panic spiked through her.

"I'm good. Can you move?"

"Yes." She barely got the word out when he hauled her up.

"We've got to go then." His hand wrapped around hers, and he started to pull her forward. She stumbled a couple steps as her mind kicked into gear.

"What about the bike?"

"The front tire's toast."

The knowledge brought reality flooding back of the security chief and his flunky, the helicopter and the shot. Marley broke into a run, ignoring the protesting aches of her body, as Zan matched his pace to hers. Behind them they could hear a vehicle brake. Another shot rang out as they dodged and wove through the trees.

Wood splintered off a tree not far from her head.

Marley ducked reflexively and kept going. She put on more speed, getting into the rhythm of the stride. The throbbing in her head matched her footfalls on the ground, but she didn't slow.

They broke through the trees and skidded to a stop at the sight of the helicopter hovering just in front of them. Zan tugged her hand. They switched direction only to have the white security vehicle come over the rise directly into their path followed by one of the infamous black SUVs.

"Put your hands up." The voice coming through the speaker on the helicopter had a surreal sound to it, but it was the gun pointed at them by the man through the helicopter's open door that made her stop and raise her hands over her head.

Beside her, Zan slowly followed the motion. Marley was afraid that he would go for his gun and knew they would shoot him. She picked up a shift in his stance. He was like a coil ready to spring.

"Zan?"

"Just do what they say."

Marley had to force her gaze from him. As she did, fear rose within her.

The security guard Jansen, stepped from the van and sauntered toward her, his gun cradled across his body, an unholy gleam in his eyes. "Why, Dr. Reynolds, who would have guessed?" He looked her up and down.

"Cut it out," Calvin Mills snapped at Jansen, but his attention was fixed on Zan. "Very carefully remove your weapons and throw them over there." He motioned with the tip of his gun and waited while Zan complied. "Now, remove your helmets."

Marley waited for Zan then followed his example. In slow, careful movements, she undid the straps and pulled the helmet off. As soon her hair was free, the draft from the helicopter whipped it around her face. Marley shook back her hair which sent her head to pounding harder. She swayed slightly.

"Freeze." The demand from Mills startled her.

She realized Zan had reached to steady her.

"Back away from her. Do it." Mills barked out the order when Zan was slow to react.

"Just shoot him." Jansen sneered.

"No!" Marley moved to stand in front of Zan.

"Marley," Zan snapped.

"Hold it right there, Doc."

Marley knew she liked the way Zan called her Doc better than Jansen.

"Take three steps to the left or we will put a hole in Masters." Mills ordered.

Terror boiled inside her threatening to make her sick. Marley raised her hands again in submission, slid one foot to the side, she shifted then repeated the process two more times.

"Down on your knees, Masters. Nice and slow," the security chief instructed.

A shiver coursed through her as Zan dropped to the ground.

"Cross your ankles," Jansen snapped with a touch of glee.

Zan glared but followed the order.

"That's good. Now, Dr. Reynolds, real careful, take off the backpack and throw it over here," Mills directed her, still keeping his attention focused on Zan.

Marley unhooked the pack, removing it from her shoulders, and gave it a light toss so it dropped halfway between them.

He ignored the pack, looking back at her. "Now if you'll kindly tell us where the information you copied is."

Marley knew instinctively that as soon as they had the information, she and Zan were dead. What she didn't know was why they hadn't shot them yet after trying to do so a couple times already. Her gaze settled on the helicopter still hovering off the ground just thirty feet away and she had her answer. The men on the helicopter weren't with Mills which meant they were witnesses who would ask questions.

Bolstered, Marley looked directly at Mills. "H-hidden in a safe place where you c-can't get it."

Jansen scoffed, striding toward her, the gleam on his face intensifying. "Oh, you'll tell us. Women always tell their lovers." He reached out to grab the front of her shirt.

Jansen's fingers barely closed on the material when Zan moved. He rolled and flipped to his feet so fast Marley missed most of the action. A gurgle escaped Jansen's throat as Zan locked on him. Zan broke Jansen's hold on her, and she stumbled back. Jansen tried to throw a punch back at Zan, but Zan deflected it with ease and threw Jansen to the ground.

"Run, Marley," Zan yelled. Instead of following her, he turned to meet Jansen as the security guard rolled, coming back up to his feet and charging Zan like an angry bull. Zan groaned as Jansen caught him in his injured shoulder. The two clashed together, but it was obvious Zan had him on strength and skill.

Marley forced herself to run but she only made it a few steps before she heard the crack of the shot as a bullet whizzed past her head. Marley froze and turned in time to see the man in the open helicopter door fire. This shot wasn't directed at her, nor was it fired high.

"Zan." Her warning came too late as Zan was hit in the back as he struggled with Jansen.

"Nooo!"

Zan jerked but continued to fight a second longer before he dropped to one knee then toppled to the ground, revealing the dart hanging from his shoulder.

Standing over him, Jansen sucked in a breath a second before he drew back his leg and sent his booted-foot into Zan's side.

"No." Marley rushed Jansen, throwing herself on the

man before he could deliver another kick. She clawed and scratched at his face.

"Why you." His blow hit Marley on the cheek, knocking her to the ground next to Zan's still body.

It took her a minute to catch her breath and shake the fog from her mind. "Zan." She crawled the two feet to his body, tears blurring her vision. "Zan." She ripped the dart from his shoulder, leaning over to check his breathing. To her relief, his pulse was strong.

"Really, Miss Reynolds." The voice of Dr. Oscar Hymas brought her attention up. "Most unprofessional of you."

Marley rested Zan's head in her lap and glared at the rat-faced doctor who had stepped out of the SUV with a man in a military uniform she didn't recognize.

When she remained silent, Hymas turned to the military man. "Why don't you call off the helicopter? We can handle them from here on out."

Again, Marley got the feeling they didn't want any more witnesses than necessary or maybe the chance someone would hear what she had to say.

The officer stared at them for several seconds. "I agree."

Marley studied him while he spoke into a microphone. She guessed him to be in his early forties. His brown hair was buzzed military short. He was handsome but had an arrogant look about him.

The door on the helicopter closed then the copter rose and flew off.

"There now, let's get some restraints on them. Masters should be out for a while, but we don't want to take any chances."

"I say we just shoot him," Jansen grumbled, obviously knowing he had no say.

The officer sent a scowl at Hymas. "Yes and we've seen what your ideas have led to, an all-out manhunt. From now on you follow my orders. Restrain him."

"N-no." Marley wrapped her arms over Zan's chest, pulling him closer as Mills and Jansen approached. When they reached to drag him away, she attacked, catching Drew Jansen in his already flat face with her fist. To her surprise, she heard a popping sound and blood gushed from his nose. Before she could do anything else, Mills wrapped his arms around her, pinning her arms down and squeezing the air from her.

"I think she broke my nose," Jansen whined, his hand covering his nose and mouth. Fire filled his eyes, and he stepped toward her.

"Mills, control your man," the officer barked. His hand came up from his side with a pistol in it, but instead of it being pointed at her it was aimed at the security chief's second in command.

"Drew!"

The bleeding man had already frozen at the sight of the gun.

"Go get cleaned up," Mills ordered.

Anger flowed off Jansen as he turned to the security vehicle. Marley didn't have time to worry about him as Mills grabbed one arm and pulled it around her back, then the other, locking her wrists in one hand as she felt a tight cord cinch around them. He then forced her to her knees before turning his attention to Zan.

She wanted to cry when Mills yanked Zan's left arm back. Though Zan hadn't said anything about it bothering him, she knew it had to hurt, and even though he was unconscious now, the rough treatment would cause him pain later.

That wasn't what would bother Zan most, though. After all his efforts, they'd been caught.

"Now, Miss Reynolds." Dr. Hymas walked to stand over her. "We will ask again. What did you do with the information you copied? And don't try to deny it."

"W-where you can't f-find it." Her stuttering was back. "Ev-ven with us, it w-will go to the authorities." *Did that sound lame?* She stiffened her shoulders and glared at him.

"I think." The military man stepped forward. "We should take this to the yard."

There was a second's hesitation in Hymas before he nodded. "You're quite right." A gleam came into his eyes. "I know how curious Miss Reynolds is, and we can always use more subjects." He turned and walked back to the SUV. "Get them loaded," he said over his shoulder.

Chapter Twelve

Marley was forced to sit on the ground. The officer stood over her as Zan was searched, then Jansen joined Mills and together they dragged Zan to the black SUV and stuffed him into the back cargo area. When that was done, she was directed to stand.

"I want a turn," Jansen commented as the military man patted her down.

Marley shuddered at the thought, actually grateful when the officer led her to the SUV and sat her in the backseat. Even before the door closed, she turned to look back at Zan. There was no sign of him stirring, but she could make out his chest raising and falling steadily.

Marley wanted to cry. Once again, it hit her that it was all her fault. First, he was shot, and now he was being taken to be killed. She had no doubt of the outcome. Marley just didn't know what she could do to stop it, and at the moment, with Zan unconscious, there was nothing he could do to protect himself.

The vision of Jansen kicking him came to her mind. She couldn't even reach Zan to check if he'd broken a rib. A single tear tickled down her cheek before she could stop it and stiffen her resolve. She had to think, figure out something to save them. It was up to her now.

Before she could come up with anything, they hit a hard bump. Her head smacked against the window and she fell off the seat to the floor. Pain and darkness swam around her already pounding head.

For a moment, she thought she'd be sick. By the time the nausea cleared, they were back on smooth road. She wiggled her way onto the seat, leaning once more over the back as much to keep an eye on Zan as for balance and the fact it was more comfortable with her hands fastened behind her.

Fear ate at her, but she lowered her head onto the seat, dividing her attention between Zan and watching out the window. They cleared the mountain road only to follow a series of smaller roads through lower hills.

By the clock on the dash, nearly an hour and a half passed before they turned into a drive that led to a large gate and a fence that had to be at least ten feet tall with wicked-looking barbwire curled at the top. Mills got out of the security vehicle in front of them and opened the gate. Marley watched him refasten the padlock after they drove through. They followed the road at least a half mile before coming to an old house with a sagging porch, a separate garage and a huge, gray metal Quonset hut.

They parked in front of the metal building, but Marley's attention locked on what looked like an arena beside it. She knew it was some kind of obstacle course because of the climbing platforms and ropes dangling from poles that had to be a good forty feet tall. What she couldn't see but knew were there were barbwire obstacles to crawl under and go through, clubs, dummies and an assortment of things that Marley didn't know what they were.

It wasn't the course or the items in it that disturbed her, but the memories of the video clips Galen Bone had sent her of men on the Gladiator drug going through the course. Men had killed and died there.

She was so wrapped up in the memory that she jumped when the officer grabbed her arm and hauled her out of the car.

"Get him out and lock him up. We want him awake for this," the military man said to the two security men then pulled her toward the metal Quonset door Dr. Hymas was unlocking.

Inside, the building was sectioned off. There was a large fighting-cage made of wire extending all the way to the ceiling in the middle that Marley again recognized from the video clips. On one side of the building, several rooms had been constructed. Marley was led to one door and guessed behind one of the others would be a lab with its exam table. She shuddered.

At the sound of a clank behind her, she turned to see Zan being dragged in. She was yanked back around before she could get a good look at him. She tried to pull away but was too late. The door in front of her was opened, and she was shoved inside.

The door banged closed behind her as she fell to the concrete floor. She hit hard unable to catch herself or do anything to soften the landing with her hands behind her back. There was another bang that reverberated through the metal building, and she figured Zan was being dumped in another room. She wished they could've been together.

Marley got to her feet and studied the room, not that she had much hope of escaping even if her hands weren't tied. There was a cot on one side, but that was all except the bare-bulb light overhead. After a dozen trips around the eight-by-ten room, she sank down on the cot and groaned in frustration.

C33ED

Zan fought to pull himself out of the fog that surrounded his brain. It took him several seconds to take in his surroundings. He lay on cold cement. When he tried to move, he found his hands tied behind his back with plastic fasteners. His shoulder throbbed. He tried to bring up his last mission and froze.

Marley! He turned his head to look for her only to find

the tiny, austere room devoid of everything but a military issue cot.

He rolled to one knee then had to stop to catch his breath before he could make it to his feet. Tranquilizer dart, he knew the feeling and that it would pass quickly. What he didn't know was what had transpired while he was unconscious.

Where he was and what was happening all took the backseat in his mind to worrying about Marley. Was she close? Was she okay? Nothing else mattered to him but her. It only took one survey around the room to know escape was not likely. Still, he made a second go around, calculating every possibility out in his mind.

The first thing was to get his hands free. It took close examination of the cot to find a sharp edge. Pain lashed through his shoulder with each drag across the bar. The band cut into his wrist, but he ignored it. Zan had no time to cover his actions when the door swung open.

"Figured you'd be awake," a man in military dress with the insignia of a major said from the doorway. The gun in his hand let Zan know he wasn't there to help.

"Let me guess." Zan got to his feet. "Major Snyder."

There was only a brief look of surprise on the man's face. "Very good, Masters. Now if you'll come this way."

Zan shrugged, keeping his movements nonchalant as he walked toward the man who moved back as he approached. Zan took in the building in a single glance. The first thing he noticed, there was no sign of Marley. The wire mesh fighting cage gave him a moment's pause. It had to be at least thirty feet square and ran almost to the ceiling.

Two men stood in the center of the floor over what used to be his backpack. The contents were strung out, most torn apart or shredded. He saw Marley's suede-leather jacket off to one side. Ignoring it, he turned his attention to the two men. From Marley's description, Zan guessed they were the security guards from the lab. Beside them was a small weasel-faced man who would be the head of the Gladiator program.

Standing by the wall on either side of the door were two men that Zan figured were from the other SUV. Zan recognized the military stance, and though they were dressed in camo, he figured them for ex-military.

Both had rigid buzz cuts. One was as tall as he was with hard muscle. He probably did two hundred pushups every morning for a warm-up. The other was shorter but looked no less tough.

Zan knew the type, gung-ho, couldn't leave the military behind. They needed the structure, lived and breathed the authority and control. These two took it over the top with the need for violence, domination and the drive to win. He wondered if something linked to that was why they were out of the military, because it sure wouldn't be by their own choice.

"So what do you think of our camp? Major Atkins and Captain Rees," Major Snyder tilted his head to the two by the door, "have set up the perfect facility. They run an excellent weekend camp and have been very apt in finding volunteers for the testing."

Zan arched his eyebrow and gave a skeptical look. "Volunteers?"

"You'd be surprised at how many men don't ask questions at the promise of sharper, heightened reactions."

"Especially when you convince them the military is using it," Zan added.

The man shrugged.

Zan looked around the area then back to the major. "And how did you explain so many of the weekend warriors dropping dead?"

"Simple coronaries. The men were not as fit as they claimed."

"And the ones that went berserk? Or are you going to deny that?"

"Some of the guys we get off the street are not very stable."

"Off the street. So what, you promise them some good meals and a place to stay and maybe even a little money if they fill in as extras in your war games."

Snyder showed pause. "Very good, Lieutenant Colonel Masters," he emphasized the rank. "Now, if you'd make your way over here." Snyder motioned with the tip of his gun.

As Zan got closer, it was obvious the one security guard had a newly broken nose. Not that it affected his looks, but Zan couldn't remember hitting him in the fight.

"That's good. Now if you'll just stay still. Remember, I won't hesitate to shoot you if you try anything," Snyder motioned, and the security chief approached him.

A chain attached to an eye-bolt cemented in the floor was run up between Zan's zip-tied arms and fastened, effectively staking him in place. Zan used the time to send his gaze around the area one more time.

He only saw the six men. There was always the possibility of others but the more he thought about it, he didn't think so. The more people that knew about what they were doing, the greater the chance of someone getting a conscience or letting what was going on slip. Then again, Mills and Jansen were probably just paid flunkies, and the other two hired muscle, or they had a payback grudge against the military, which was a distinct possibility.

"I don't suppose you would consider telling us where the information Dr. Reynolds copied is?" Major Snyder looked at him directly.

Zan focused back on the man, cocked up one side of his mouth into a crocked smile and said nothing.

"I didn't think so after checking your file. But there are other ways to get the information." Snyder walked across the floor to another door. "It's really too bad you had to get involved. You've had quite a distinguished career. Dr.

Reynolds picked an appropriate champion." He released the lock and swung open the door.

Zan could only see into half the room that looked identical to the one he'd been held in. Marley was nowhere in sight then she stepped into the doorway. She looked frightened but fine. For a moment, he felt weak with relief then his determination began to build. He had to get them out of there.

Marley saw him and started toward him only to have Snyder catch her arm and jerk her to a stop. Pain wiped out the relief Zan saw in her face. He saw the exact instant she saw the chain holding him and shock took over. She got a wide-eyed look and stumbled in her step, visibly more shaken.

"Over here." Snyder jerked her arm again, pulling her forward. Before she had time to comply, she tripped and would've gone down, but Snyder hauled her back onto her feet.

They stopped on the other side of the strung out backpack. "Now, Dr. Reynolds, since we've already made introductions out here," Snyder began. "I think we'll just start with, where is the information you took from the lab? And what was on it?"

For a minute, Marley said nothing. Jansen stepped up behind Zan and jabbed him in the back. Fire burst through his body. Zan hissed out. Marley screamed. Almost as soon as the pain started, it stopped.

"Good old fashioned cattle-prod." The gloating voice came from behind him, and there was a smacking sound of something hitting flesh. Zan didn't need to turn to know Jansen was smacking the prod against his palm to taunt Marley.

Marley went ashen, but Zan had to give her credit for not looking at the backpack or her jacket. If they were still asking it meant they hadn't found it, which was the only reason he and Marley were still alive.

"Shall I ask again? Let's start with an easy question. What was the information Dr. Bone sent you to make you go running off?"

Zan heard a rustling behind him and saw Marley's eyes widen. "Everyth-thing." She stuttered in her hurry to get the word out. The shock didn't come, but Zan flinched for Marley. He didn't want to see the stuttering come back.

"Now that was easy," Snyder mocked her. "Why don't you tell us exactly?"

At the remark, Marley glanced at the major and straightened, meeting his gaze right on. "How you are k-killing men and c-covering it up, falsifying d-data to mask the truth. That you are g-going to send it out, no m-matter the lives you're r-risking."

"Dr. Hymas was afraid Boney had it all figured out. I guess he was right."

"There was v-video of men dying, bleeding to death, killing thems-selves."

The man didn't even acknowledge her comment. "Should've handled him sooner, but I didn't think he had the guts to act." The major looked her up and down. "Though, I guess he really didn't. Now, if you will just tell me where the information is?"

Zan barely made a sideways motion with his head when Marley flicked her gaze to him. The jolt hit his back. He was ready for it this time but couldn't control jerking away. The chains rattled holding him in place, but he made no sound.

Zan could see Marley's eyes swim with tears.

"She doesn't know. I have it," Zan hissed out between trying to catch his breath. "I already called it in and sent the information to a friend. I'm afraid your little secret's out."

The major shifted to look at him. "Nice try, but we've been monitoring your phones. Even the little side one you picked up." He pulled it from his pocket, held it up then opened his fingers and let it fall to the concrete. There was a cracking sound and one piece flew off, but Snyder wasn't finished. Lifting his booted foot, he brought it down hard, crushing the phone.

"You want to try again?" He turned back to Marley.

"Might I suggest," Oscar Hymas broke in. "It seems if Miss Reynolds has taken on such interest in Gladiator, that maybe it would be wise to let her see it firsthand. After all, as I said earlier, we can always use another test subject. It has been somewhat hard to get good candidates, and Lieutenant Colonel Masters is perfect, right down to his experience."

"No," Marley went to charge him only to be pulled back by Snyder. She cried out when he jerked up on her arms.

Behind him, Zan heard Jansen snicker.

"The idea has merit. What do you suggest?" Snyder said thoughtfully as if the idea hadn't already come to him.

The doctor was quiet a second. "First, I think we should put Miss Reynolds in the cage. After all, I'm sure she really wouldn't want to miss this."

Snyder nodded and motioned to the door. Atkins walked toward them.

"No." Marley pulled back as he approached. "You can't do this." She rammed her shoulder into Snyder almost taking him down before he caught his balance. Marley wasn't so fortunate. She went down. Her head hitting Snyder's foot was the only thing that kept it from striking the floor. She remained down, dazed but still conscious.

"Marley!" Zan pulled against the restraints, not caring how futile the attempt. He wanted to get to her.

"How touching," Jansen mocked, just before he jabbed the cattle prod in his side one more time.

Zan clenched his teeth and twisted to the side, catching hold of the end of the device. He continued to twist, ripping the prod from the security guard's hands. Zan then changed directions, swung out his leg, catching the man at the ankles, swiping his feet out from under him. Zan came down on him with his knee on Jansen's chest.

"Don't touch her, or he dies." Zan edged his knee closer to Jansen's throat until the man made a gagging sound. Zan knew, with his hands fastened the way they were behind his back, his threat wouldn't work, so he was surprised when Snyder halted Atkins in his reach for Marley.

"Very nice move, but since Dr. Reynolds has already taken Mr. Jansen down and broke his nose, I can't be too impressed. So if you want, you can go ahead and kill him, but I do wonder how you would fare against Atkins and Rees."

Zan's first thought was how it was Marley had broken the man's nose, accompanied with a sense of pride in her. He then locked onto what he was being offered. Number one, it would buy them some time. Greater still, it was a chance to get his hands free, and maybe he could do something to free them. One on one, he figured he could take the men, but he knew that was not what was being offered. The big thing was to avoid being given the drug.

"My hands free?" Zan decided to see exactly what he could get.

Snyder nodded.

"No drug."

Again the major nodded.

"What about using him as a subject?" Hymas burst out.

"If he loses, he'll be given the drug," Snyder said, and Zan didn't doubt the man was certain he would lose. "It will be a much more viable test with a base to start. With his and Dr. Reynolds' lives on the line, he will have greater motivation."

"But if he wins?" There was a whine in the doctor's voice.

"Will he win, gentlemen?" Snyder's gaze remained locked on Zan as the two men shook their heads.

"Your call Lieutenant Colonel"

"Zan." Worry touched Marley's voice and wavered in her eyes.

"I'll fight," Zan said coolly.

"Excellent. First things first. I think we need to find a good seat for Dr. Reynolds."

Zan kept Jansen pinned down while Snyder and Atkins helped Marley up. Not that he really held any leverage in the action. It was all show. Atkins led Marley to a four row high metal bleachers on one end of the cage, while Snyder walked to a workbench not far away.

"I think we can change Dr. Reynolds' hands to in front of her." He picked up a pair of handcuffs and tossed them to the man, who caught them with one hand while reaching down to remove a wicked looking knife from a sheath strapped to his thigh.

Zan's breath caught as Atkins brought it up, but he simply sliced through the band at Marley's wrist with an effortless stroke. A groan escaped Marley as she brought her hands around in front of her to rub her wrists. The man actually gave her a minute before demanding her wrists to put the handcuffs on and forced her to sit down.

"Now, Colonel Masters." The major motioned to the cage.

Zan got to his feet, waited as they released the chain. He walked slowly toward the cage, keeping an eye on all the men in the room. Jansen stayed down, his hand going to his throat. Rees remained by the door, the gun in his hand a subtle warning not to try to escape. Not that it was needed. Zan wasn't going anywhere without Marley. Atkins met him at the cage entrance, opening it for him to pass through.

Zan heard Marley's hiss of breath as he stepped in. He turned back, sending her a look that he hoped would reassure her. Atkins followed him. Rees crossed the floor, paused to place his gun on the same bench that Snyder had picked up the handcuffs from before entering the cage, confirming Zan's suspicions of not being allowed to face them one at a time.

Mills came over to secure the opening. He turned and nodded to Snyder, who glanced toward Hymas at a control panel, activating what Zan guessed, was the recording equipment.

"Ready?" Hymas asked.

"Wait," Marley interrupted. "Their knives, they're still armed and you haven't freed him."

Atkins smiled like a snake, sliding his knife from its sheath, turning it side to side so the blade reflected the light. "Wrists," he said.

Zan held them away from his body as he shifted to the side while keeping an eye on the man. The blade slid through the restraint as easily as it had cut Marley's, but it was lucky he was watching because, as soon as it cleared his wrist, Atkins arched it around, slicing out at him.

Zan heard Marley's cry, but he was already spinning out of the way of the blade which missed him only by a quarter of an inch. Zan kept going to the left, so his back was in the corner and neither man could get behind him. While the two men separated, each going wide to opposite sides in a well-practiced move, Zan rolled his shoulders and rubbed his wrist to ease the stiffness in them. Stiffness right then could be deadly.

Rees was the first to come in, swinging out in a distraction move that Zan was ready for. Zan blocked, countered the hit, catching the man in the side with enough force to knock the air from him, and continued around to meet Atkins' attack from the other side.

Atkins had replaced the knife, coming at him with fists. Zan caught the punch, deflecting his hand up as he turned, sending his elbow back into the ex-military man's chest. Zan still had his hands locked on Atkins when he kicked out at Rees. He caught the man full in the stomach dropping him to the ground.

Atkins hit him in the side, and Zan dodged, barely missing a kick that would have taken out his knee. He spun, and they came together in a succession of punches. Out of the corner of his eye, Zan saw Rees rush in. Zan sidestepped and the man's momentum carried him into Atkins who hadn't noticed him coming. Both men went down.

Zan staggered to the opposite corner of the cage, gulping in air. His shoulder was on fire again. He brushed the sweat from his brow with the back of his hand. Zan watched as the men got to their feet, coming at him more cautiously.

Instead of dividing, they came in with a concentrated attack. Blows rained from all sides and though he was out of practice, Zan's training served him well. He met Atkins' strike and countered Rees at the same time, sending his fist into Rees' neck. Rees backpedaled, saving him from an incapacitating blow.

Atkins wrapped his arms around Zan, effectively pinning him down. Zan struggled, trying to throw him off. When that didn't work, Zan planted his feet and pushed back, slamming them into the fence. Zan thrust back again then spun forward, throwing Atkins to the ground.

Zan let his motion carry him around, barely missing the swipe of the knife in Rees' hand. Zan forced his gaze from the blade to watch Rees' movements instead. When Rees lunged, Zan was ready, knocking Rees' hand up then wrapped his hands around to lock onto Rees' wrist, twisting it over.

Rees cried out and released the knife. Zan continued to force him over and down to the ground then sent his fist into the man's face. Rees dropped unconscious to the concrete. Zan snatched up the knife as he dove and rolled to his feet, moving back as Atkins slid his own knife from its sheath.

Chapter Thirteen

Marley fought to keep from screaming when she saw the shorter man stagger to his feet and pull his knife. She knew if she cried out it could be a fatal distraction to Zan, but her fear almost got the better of her when the man struck at Zan. Marley didn't know how Zan was able to block the knife, but in a blurring string of movement, he had the man to the ground and the man's knife.

The only place she had ever seen anyone fight like that was the movies, but she knew the blood that trickled down at the corner of Zan's lip was real.

When the other man turned on him pulling his knife, Marley felt as if her heart would stop. Cold rage shot from the man. If he could kill Zan, he would. Atkins slashed out setting off another flurry of movements. Marley held her breath, afraid that any moment the razor sharp metal would slice through Zan's skin or would be wedged deep into his body.

Tears spiked in her eyes when the blade ripped through the front of Zan's shirt and blood colored the area. Zan made no reaction to pain, slashing out to leave two similar marks on the man. Both men were breathing hard, circling, making small jabs that she figured were to either to distract or test the other. When Aktins attacked, Zan was ready, countering the move, knocking the knife away.

"Freeze." The order cut through the air, halting Zan in mid-strike.

Marley had been so wrapped up in the fight that it wasn't until Zan started to turn her direction that she realized Snyder had moved in behind her. She jerked as she felt the circle of cold metal brush her temple. A hand clamped down on her arm with bruising strength.

"Drop the knife." The demand came low and forceful so close to her ear, Marley felt the air stir the hair on her neck.

Tears burned her eyes as she watched Zan's fingers open, and the knife slip to the ground.

"Most impressive, Colonel Masters. I've never seen Atkins and Rees bested. But I'm afraid I must change the rules of the game. Over in the corner."

Zan complied slowly, going to the corner just left of Marley. His chest rose and fell with the depth of his breathing. He raised his forearm to wipe the sweat from his brow but his eyes were fixed on her with hot intent.

"Check on Rees," Snyder ordered.

Atkins staggered as he moved to comply. The other man had regained consciousness. Atkins helped him to his feet.

"Mills, Jansen, get over here," the major barked out.

Jansen's eyes bore down on her as he approached. Revenge and hatred warped his already swollen, harsh face. "It looks like we're ready for the good time."

"What?" Marley's stomach clenched.

"Payback." The man sneered.

Before she could question again, Snyder spoke up. "Dr. Hymas, do you have the hypodermic ready."

"Right here." The rat faced man scurried past.

"No." Marley started to stand only to be jerked back and have the gun jabbed once more to her temple.

"Marley." Zan cautioned by just saying her name as the three men entered the cage.

"You c-can't do this," she cried but got no reaction.

Zan looked past the approaching men to Snyder. "How

are you going to explain our deaths? People will ask questions. We aren't your street people."

It was Dr. Hymas that answered. "Quite simple really. I should've thought of it earlier. If you survive the first round, we'll give you a double dose and blame it on Miss Reynolds. That she was doing some experiments on her own."

"Doc was looking for a real exciting time," Jansen cut in.

The doctor glared at him before turning back to Zan. "Yes, she gave you too much. You went berserk and killed her then yourself. It won't take much at the lab to point evidence to her."

"W-what about the information I c-copied." Marley spoke up trying to think of an arguement. Zan stood calm, but she couldn't manage it.

"With you gone, there's no problem," Snyder answered.

The men swarmed around Zan. Rees stepped forward and shoved him back against the fence. Mills and Jansen caught his right arm, while Atkins took the left. Rees shoved his forearm up under Zan's chin, forcing his head up. Beside Rees, Hymas held up the syringe, directing the tip to Zan's arm.

"No!" This time Marley screamed it at the top of her lungs and threw herself back into Snyder. Her head caught him square in the face and, for the second time that day, she heard a sickening pop just before they toppled off the bleachers. Marley landed on top of the man who remained still beneath her.

In the ring attention shifted for a brief second, but it was all Zan needed. He brought his knee up, dropping Rees. Jerking his right arm up, he lifted Mills a couple inches off the ground and jabbed his elbow into Jansen's face, catching him in his already broken nose. The guard howled and collapsed. Zan felt the prick of the needle in his arm just as he swung Mills into the doctor. They both went down.

Atkins landed two punches in his side before Zan turned to the man. They traded several more blows before they staggered back. Atkins barreled in, driving Zan back against the wire.

Zan brought his arms up breaking the hold, jabbing an elbow into the man's neck muscle, followed immediately with a fist to his stomach. As the man doubled over, Zan locked his hands behind Atkins' neck and smashed his face into the knee he drove up. Atkins dropped limp to the floor.

"Zan."

Zan looked up to find Marley in the cage, the syringe in her hand. Fear on her face. The syringe wasn't empty but about half the liquid was gone. Zan wanted to say it had just been injected out, but he could already feel it burning in his bloodstream. Before he could say anything the doors burst open. Men carrying weapons, dressed in camo and helmets poured into the building.

Marley let out a little shriek and spun. "Not more," she cried out.

"Marley, get your hands up," Zan ordered, as he locked his hands behind his neck. "It's okay. These are on our side."

The men fanned out as they came toward the cage, surveying the scene. "Colonel Masters?"

"Yes."

"We were told you needed rescuing." The man eased his hold on the gun.

"We can definitely use your help." He lowered his hands, stepping over the men at his feet. He went directly to Marley though talking to the soldiers. "All these men need to be taken into custody."

Marley reached for him, wrapping her arms around him. He pulled her tight, losing all thought of what he was saying the instant he came in contact with her.

"It's all right." Zan buried his face in her hair. The sweet, spicy smell of her was intoxicating. He brushed his lips across her neck and wanted more, wanted all.

It took him only a second to realize what was happening to him. He pushed her back. "The drug."

"He jabbed you?" It was as much a statement as a question. Her gaze skimmed over him.

Zan nodded.

"About h-half what was in there is gone. I don't know what they consider a full d-dose." She reached up to brush his cheek then placed her fingers to his neck to take his pulse.

"Marley." He pushed her hand away. "Don't touch me."

"What?" She looked confused, reaching for his wrist.

"The drug, I can feel it in my system. Don't touch me. I don't want to hurt you." He shook his arm free, catching her wrist then dropping it.

"You wouldn't," she said with confidence, reaching for him again.

"I don't know that," he ground out, stepping back away from her.

"I do. I need to monitor your vitals."

"No." Sweat broke out on his brow at the thought of her touching him. "I need you to move farther away. I'm feeling a little … lustful right now." He took a deep breath and even at the distance between them, the smell of her filled him again. He fought to control his flooding desire.

Marley must have finally recognized his struggle because she pulled back. Her gaze locked on him, but she stepped out of the cage. "Is there a medic?" There was a tremor in her words, but she didn't stumble over them.

"Here, ma'am." A man came forward.

Marley turned to him but her gaze kept flickering back to Zan. "You have to monitor Zan's, Colonel Master's, vitals. He was injected with the Gladiator drug. It over stimulates the system. It can send the person into an uncontrollable, violent rage or cause a coronary. I don't believe he was given a full does. But I don't know how much they had in the needle. He would know." She pointed to Dr. Hymas.

The medic nodded his understanding and entered the cage, going past the other soldiers working to detain Snyder and Hymas's crew.

"Dr. Reynolds?" A man approached her.

"Yes."

"I'm Captain Williams, if you'll come with me. You're to be taken in for debriefing."

Marley looked back at Zan. The medic was checking his vitals, but Zan's gaze was lock on her.

"Go with him," Zan said to her.

Her desire to return to Zan was almost overpowering. Only the knowledge that she was causing him discomfort had her stepping away. Still she paused and turned back.

"Go," he growled through clinched teeth.

She felt the tug on her heart. With reluctance, she nodded and let the captain lead her out of the building. Marley was surprised to see the sun was starting to set. She couldn't believe all that had happened in a single day.

"If you'll wait right here, they'll bring a vehicle up for you," the captain said to her, easing her to the center of the yard.

She didn't have anything to do but study the area. A shiver went through her. The place felt tainted to her, but she knew it was just her imagination filling in what she knew had happened there. An SUV so similar to the black ones that had hounded them pulled up, and Marley felt another wave of trepidation, though this one carried a military insignia on the side. The captain started to direct her to it when Zan stepped from the building with a medic.

She turned to him. "How is he?" she directed her question to the medic.

"His vitals are elevated but holding steady," the medic assured her.

"I'm okay," Zan added.

Marley ignored the way he tried to brush the threat away. "Watch him. That drug has killed at least a dozen men." She waited until she received a nod from the man before she looked at Zan, unable to hold back her tears. "You make sure they take care of you. I mean it, Zan."

A harsh oath cut from him. He strode to her, hauled her up against him, kissed her savagely then pushed her away. "Get her out of here." He locked his hands together behind his back. His shoulders and arms muscles bulged with restraint. The fire that burned in his eyes took her breath. She hurried and climbed into the vehicle not in fear but in effort to ease some of the stress that radiated off him.

The officer shut the door behind her and waved to the vehicle away. Marley couldn't take her eyes off Zan as the SUV drove off. At her last glimpse of him, he still stood in the center of the yard, staring after her. The medic had a hand on his arm talking to him, but Zan looked like warrior statue illuminated by the setting sun.

Exhausted, Marley laid her head on the rest, closed her eyes and tucked the image of Zan in her heart, wrapped in the knowledge that she loved him. Somewhere along the way to wherever they took her, she fell asleep. She woke as they came to a stop at a guard post and a high-powered flashlight hit her in the face. Marley hardly got her hand up to block the beam before it was gone and they were driving through.

A few minutes later, after several turns they pulled up to a large, four-story, cinderblock building, she was ushered out of the SUV, up the stairs and inside. There began the introductions to numerous military officers, of varying high ranks with whom she went over her story, only to answer a string of question and repeat all that happened again.

Marley was reassured so many times that, "Colonel Masters was doing fine. That he was under medical supervision and also being debriefed", she wanted to scream. What she really wanted was Zan.

She understood the need for all the details of what happened, but it didn't help her fear for Zan. Marley was ready to plead for just a single minute to see for herself that he was all right, when they finally called a halt to the questioning.

"May I see Colonel Masters now?" she asked the two men who escorted her from the room. There was a silence. Marley thought for a moment they weren't going to answer her then the two exchanged glances, and the taller of the two looked down at her.

"I'm sorry ma'am, but it isn't allowed."

"I'm a doctor. I want to check and make sure he is all right." Marley tried imposing another angle.

"Colonel Masters has received medical treatment," the man answered back plainly.

Marley knew he was trying to reassure her but it wasn't helping. She bit back the threatening explosion and wondered how much trouble she'd get in if she punched him in the nose. She sighed heavily knowing she couldn't do that to him. He was just trying to help and was being very pleasant.

"Where are we going then?" Marley gave up and asked.

"We're to escort you to your room." The words were hardly out of his mouth when they stop in front of a door, and he reached over and opened it. "You can stay here tonight. We'll be out here on guard."

"G-guard? I, I'm under a-arrest? I hav-ven't done anything wrong." Marley felt a wave of panic and her fear for Zan surge.

"Relax," the shorter man spoke up quickly. "You're not in trouble." There was a slight drawl to his words.

"We're just to make sure nothin' happens to you. You're safe. Don't you worry, so is Colonel Masters." He tacked on the end.

Marley wasn't sure if it was the down-home honesty in his voice, or that exhaustion finally burned out the last of her energy, but she did relax. "Thank you," she got out, her whole body becoming numb.

"If there's anything you need just let us know," the taller guard said.

Marley was tempted to say Zan and the thought must have shown on her face because the shorter soldier shook his head.

"I can't do that. Anything else?" A smile accompanied the drawl.

This time it was Marley that shook her head and she closed the door, leaning back against it. She was ready to drop but her anxiety over Zan kicked in and she started pacing the room.

Had the drug had worked its way out of his system? Was he all right? What about his shoulder? Was he close?

Marley tried to convince herself that if something was wrong someone surely they would have told her, but she wasn't really positive that was the case. She wasn't his wife or even his girlfriend as far as they knew. Who would believe that they could build a relationship in four days?

She went to the window and looked out, subconsciously hoping to see Zan looking out another window, but no such luck. Marley dropped her head to the glass and the tears started to make their way free.

She wanted Zan. She wanted him to hold her and she wanted to hold him. Take care of him and make him better.

Fear hit her deep. After all the pain and trouble she'd caused him, maybe he wouldn't want her anymore. She couldn't blame him. In the time she'd known him he had to run for his life, he'd been shot, tortured and drugged twice and his house had been attacked.

All in the four short days of their time together. It seemed so much longer. It felt like she'd known him forever.

Marley finally pulled away from the window and stretched out on the bed. Burrowing in the blankets, she doubted anything would warm her. Still, she was surprised that she actually went to sleep, her thoughts lingering on Zan, focused on the memory of his kisses.

In the morning, she was given a plain blouse and skirt to wear, and after a breakfast was served to her in her room, the process was started all over again with questions and no sight of Zan. After lunch, she was taken back to the room and left for the rest of the day with the ever present guards at her door.

Frustrated, Marley tried to watch movies, but all she could think about was Zan. Again she was assured he was fine, that he had recovered fully from the effects of the drug, but it didn't help.

She wanted to yell. *Didn't they understand she was in love with him?* Her heart ached.

After another awful night of worrying and nightmares, Marley had reached the end of her endurance. As she escorted down the hall the next morning, she decided she was going to demand to see Zan. That she had rights. She was working herself up into a fevered pitch when she came around the corner and ran straight into an officer in full dress uniform, her nose bumping into the medals and ribbons on his chest. Marley started to pull back only to find herself caught by an arm around her waist. She lifted her head to protest and the words in her throat changed to a cry.

The love and fear in her burst. Marley launched herself at him. Zan caught her up, pulling her tight to his chest as she wrapped her arms around his neck. Marley hung in the air, not caring who was around, only that he was there and he was kissing her.

When they finally came up for air, she cupped his face, hardly believing she was actually in his arms. "You're okay." She brushed her fingers over his cheeks. He turned his head to kiss her hand.

"Yes," he assured, before kissing her again. Desire was heavy in his eyes when he eased her back, but she knew it had nothing to do with the drug. Something deeper flickered there, too. Before she could begin to figure out what it was the sound of a throat being cleared pulled them apart. Zan lowered her to the ground, and they turned together.

"They're ready to see you now." A woman in military dress stood a couple feet away. An approving smile twisted her lips, and she actually winked at them before opening the door.

"What's happening now?" Marley asked as Zan took her elbow, guiding her in behind the woman. Marley wanted to turn back and assure herself he was staying with her.

"A review board, I'd guess." He dipped his head close enough that his breath caressed her cheek, making her shiver in awareness.

"For what?" Marley tried to think.

"To go over everything," he said as they stepped into the room.

Along one wall, sided by flags, was a long raised bench with a row of six highly decorated people. Zan led her to stand in the middle of the room, he took a rigid, military stance beside her and Marley followed suit.

"Dr. Reynolds, Lieutenant Colonel Masters asked that we hold this with you together," an older, balding man in the middle said in the way of greeting.

Marley glanced at Zan, but he didn't look toward her, remaining at attention.

The man followed her gaze. "At ease, Colonel."

Zan's body lost some of its stiffness but he stayed

straight and tall.

The officer continued. "We want to thank you for all that you have done. Your stories have been collaborated by the evidence we found where you were detained in the forms of the microchip in your jacket, videos, including the one of the attempts on you, and other documentation. Corresponding documents were found at the lab in which you worked.

"While this matter is far from over yet, and you will still be called in to testify, it's been decided that since you both have security clearance and there is no longer a threat against you, you and Colonel Master have been cleared to go. And, on behalf of our government, and all our soldiers whose lives you may have saved, I want to add my personal thanks. What you did was very courageous. Thank you, again."

Those on the stand stood as one and saluted them before coming around personally to shake hands and talk. It was another half hour before Zan drew her away.

"Come on." Zan grabbed her hand, leading her down the hall out into the sunlight. Marley tried to stop to take a deep breath, feeling free now that it was all over, but Zan propelled her down the step toward a car waiting at the curb.

"Where are we going?" She broke off, hurrying to keep up with him. "Whose car is this?"

"A rental. I had one ordered for us until we can get the motorcycle fixed." He sent a grin over his shoulder, not breaking his pace.

"Wait, Zan, we've been through this." She tried to dig in her feet but didn't even slow him down. "You can't just drag me all over the place. Where are we going?"

"To get married," he said, again not breaking his stride.

"What!" She stopped only for him to pull her forward. "We can't get married."

That stopped him, and he turned so abruptly she plowed into him. His arms snaked around her, easing her against him. "Do you love me?" he demanded as one hand came up to cradle her face, tilting it up so their eyes met.

"Yes, but–"

His head swooped down. He kissed her firmly, cutting off any objection, leaving her breathless when he eased a couple inches away to ask his next question. "You don't want to marry me?" His eyes bore into her with need plain for her to see.

"Well, yes, but–"

Again, she was cut off, this time by a quick kiss then she was jerked forward as he started walking. "Then what's the problem?" he asked over his shoulder. "I love you, you love me. The only way I can keep an eye on you is to marry you. And I think I'd better watch you. Two broken noses, Doc. Who would have guessed?"

"You love me?" Marley was stuck back at that point.

He stopped again, turned and said simply, "Yes."

Marley couldn't believe it. "You can't love me. I'm nerdy."

He laughed, reaching out to wrap his arms around her, pulling her back into him then leaning down to kiss her nose. "I happened to find nerdy very appealing. In fact, I'd like to find who convinced you, you were nerdy. First, I'd like to beat the daylights out of him and then thank him since you'll always be only mine."

"Only yours?" Joy burst inside her.

"Oh, yes." He drew it out as if savoring the word.

"You sound awfully sure of yourself."

"You love me." He shrugged his shoulders as if it was simple.

"How do you know that?"

"Besides the fact that you've admitted it, it's there every time you look at me and when you kiss me." He leaned down and kissed her hard and heated, taking away her breath. "I love you, Marley. Will you marry me?" He cupped her face, tilting her head up to him. "Marry me, please, now? I want to spend tonight and the rest of my life loving you."

"Yes." The answer came out clear, without a single tremble.

Epilogue

Marley glanced out the kitchen window to where Zan sat on the back patio, talking to her parents and brother-in-law. She couldn't believe they'd been married five days. She had to admit her parents were handling the news pretty well. Her sister, on the other hand, was not, and she was coming in for another attack.

Julie made a show of refilling her glass. "I still cannot believe that you could just go off and get married like that." The words hissed from her. "What were you thinking? You're supposed to be the smart one. You don't even know him?" Julie put her hands on her hips and struck one of her poses.

"I know everything that's important." Marley smiled, not rising to her sister's bait. Nothing her sister said could hurt her. She didn't doubt Zan's love.

Julie stared at her. "This is kind of sudden, and you don't have any experience with men." She shifted her tactic. "Especially any men like him. You hang around eggheads and nerds, not hunks with muscles."

Marley shrugged her shoulders, feeling heat bloom on her cheek as she thought of running her hands over Zan's muscles. "Zan has brains, too, and I know him. That's enough."

"Are you pregnant?" Her voice filled with accusation.

Marley didn't even pause. "No, at least I don't think so." A little trill went through her at the thought of the possibility. "We haven't even been married a week."

"You're not planning on waiting?" Her sister expression turned to one of aghast.

"We've talked about it." Marley thought about three evenings ago as they strolled on the beach not far from the little inn where they were staying in the honeymoon suite. "We'd like to have three or four children, and unless we have twins, which, I think is doubtful, we decided now is the time to start. At our ages, we don't want to wait too long."

Her sister broke in. "Why would you think of twins? We don't have twins in our family."

"No, but Zan is a twin."

Shock registered on her sister's perfect made up face. "You mean there is another one of him out there?"

Marley let her eyes lock on Zan. "No. There's only one Zan." Love filled her.

Zan caught her gaze, smiled back, rose, and strode to her. Wrapping her in his arms where she'd feel safe and loved forever.

೮ઝౠಂ

There's only one Zan, for Zac's story please join me for Mindblower.

೮ઝౠಂ

About the Author

I grew up in a small town in Wyoming loving the outdoors, sports, art, and reading Hardy Boys books. After reading them all at least a half dozen times, I started writing my own stories.

For thirty-three years I was married a wonderful, honorable man. I'm mother of five children and grandmother of nine, eight boys and one girl. I love traveling. Through my husband's work and vacations, I have visited much of the United States, all over Eastern Europe, Canada, Mexico, China, Thailand, Cambodia and Australia, giving me many intriguing locations and experiences for my stories.

I am a storyteller. I write the classic hero story because I think there's a need for more heroes, love, and adventure in our lives. I'm not out to change the world with my writing; I'm just hoping to make your day a little better.

Hope you enjoy.
Alysia S. Knight

Please feel free to visit me through my website:

www.alysiasknight.com